It's Not About
The Cookies

Inkblot Books
Vacaville, CA

It's Not About The Cookies

Published by Inkblot Books
Vacaville, California
www.inkblotbooks.com

ISBN-10: 1-932461-15-9
ISBN-13: 978-1-932461-15-2

Printed in the United States of America

Dammit, now I want cookies...

Also by K.A. Thompson

Charybdis
As Simple As That
Finding Father Rabbit

The Psychokitty Speaks Out: Diary Of A Mad Housecat
(as Max Thompson)

The Psychokitty Speaks Out: Something Of Yours Will Meet A
Toothy Death
(as Max Thompson)

Peek inside the author's head at
http://kathompson.blogspot.com

Or meet the Psychokitty at
http://psychokitty.blogspot.com

It's Not About The Cookies

~a novel

K.A. Thompson

1.

I still carry on conversations with Steven. Sometimes in my mind he has aged gracefully; he went from cute teenager to attractive young guy to handsome middle aged man. By the graces of Rogaine and Proscar he kept his hair, and he has the beginnings of that six-pack-to starter keg embraced by so many men approaching their fifties. Other times he's Goth Boy, not quite twenty, dressed in tight black clothing that matches the paint on his fingernails and the makeup rimming his eyes. In life he was never dark and miserable, but in my middle-aged brain he plays the part well. He sits at the table with me when I'm alone, when the house is empty and quiet, with the exception of a cat who feels compelled to meow at every closed door and imagined shadow.

Why, Steven wonders, *do you feel like there has to be someone to blame for all your inner demons? Most parents do the best they can, and yours were no different.*

"It's not about blame," I tell him. And it's not. Every kid limps into adulthood with a myriad of battle wounds; I simply want to figure mine out, and come to terms with why they tend to still bleed and then scab over.

That's fine, as long as you accept responsibility for your own shortcomings.

"Oh yeah, it was my fault they decided to leave you with total strangers while the rest of us moved halfway across the country. You were fifteen freaking years old. Hell, not even fifteen yet, they couldn't even hang around for your birthday."

They knew I was miserable. They knew that your mom was uncomfortable with me there. They knew Rob and Sharon would treat me like their own son, something she just couldn't do, no matter how hard she tried. And who could blame her?

"I can."

Yeah, right. If Scott came home today and said 'Well guess what? I knocked up my secretary twelve years ago and she just dropped dead, right in the middle of the Bank of America lobby with a dozen strangers staring as she hit the floor, so the bastard son we spawned is coming to live with us,' how would you feel?

"You don't abandon your kids to someone else."

You do if it's the right thing for them. Look what I got out of it. Every day I knew that when I came home from school, there were people who loved me, who wanted me there.

"I loved you. I wanted you there."

I needed parents, kiddo. I needed to not feel like an intruder.

"And you were happy with the Brownings."

Mostly. I was a teenager, after all.

"And you don't hate my parents for the way you were treated? It wasn't just those couple of years. Your own father ignored you for most of your life. He didn't fight for you."

How can I hate them? Everyone was a victim; me, you, my mother, your mother...

"But not our father."

He may have been the biggest victim of all. Don't let hurt feelings get in the way of facts. He wanted me, and he wanted me to live with his family. It wasn't as if one day he decided to throw me out with the used kitty litter. What he did was the most difficult thing he could have done to himself. He gave me a home where I'd feel wanted, even though it broke his heart.

I didn't think it had broken his heart. It seemed too easy for him; ignore the kid for twelve years, accept him for almost three, then dump him onto someone else. Leaving Steven behind cleaned up an inconvenient mess. How could his heart be broken?

He knew what it would look like, but when it got right down to it, he had to do what was the most right thing, and that was remove the reminder of his infidelity for your mother's sake, and provide a loving home for mine.

"I've never hated him, you know."

You've never hated either of them, but you don't understand them, and you blame them for that.

"Does anyone ever really understand their parents?"

I don't know. Maybe after it stops mattering so much...

"Like when you're dead."

Maybe.

"Well, they're not allowed to die until I have my own head straightened out."

Why?

"I don't know."

Because deep down, you want to be able to forgive them for their own stupidities. Because if you can't forgive them theirs, your son might not ever be able to forgive you yours.

"You're dead, dumbass. You're not allowed to play with hammers, let alone hit the nail on the head."

I know my dad loved Steven. I don't think he did the right thing. I still miss my brother deeply. I haven't heard his name uttered by anyone in my family in almost twenty five years, and I'm not sure if they've forgotten him or are simply too embarrassed to mention him.

How can you let go of the person you were supposed to outgrow stupidity with, when he never had the chance to take much more than a baby step outside of teenagedom? I'm not sure I can let him go. He's etched into my brain, and until the day I die, Steven will probably be there at my kitchen table, talking to me, making fun of me, and showing me just what an ass I really am sometimes.

2.

I get stared at a lot. Most of the time I don't mind; I understand the normalcy of curiosity, suddenly seeing someone different and needing to look, the attraction of something bright and shiny and having that impulse to touch. It's the averted glances that bother me: the sudden turn of the head, that instant where I'm magically invisible, reduced to "Oh, sorry, I didn't see you there."

I get it. I don't like it but I get it; I was also taught that it's not polite to stare. You don't want to inflict unwanted attention on someone who doesn't deserve it. And those POOR people in wheelchairs...well, gosh, we wouldn't want them to feel like FREAKS by looking at them, would we?

You'd be surprised at how people get attention, and how they try to deflect it.

Take the teenager who lives down the street. He dresses in black from head to toe, his face painted pasty white except for the thick black he's smeared onto his lips. His eyebrow piercing. The labret that screams "Yeah, I did it," seated just so between his lower lip and chin. Once in a while you see him wearing something that looks an awful lot like a studded dog collar. You can't for one moment fathom why anyone would do that to himself.

Maybe he does it so people will *stop* looking. Maybe he does it so people will look away. Maybe he wants to be anonymous.

People do that. They create these huge spectacles of themselves because deep down they understand that you'll look away. The only way they know how to be small enough to feel safe is to pop out at the world in a Screw-You kind of way.

And then there are those people who want to be noticed so desperately that they'll manipulate you in the tiniest ways to whip up the biggest effect. Give a compliment here, share a secret there. To your face they make you feel incredibly special, so special that you don't see the knife headed for your back; all you feel is a starburst of pain with the trailing thought of "What the—?"

I'm not trying to deflect anyone's attention. Neither am I trying to cultivate it. I just want to be.

I'm also realistic. I can't be the casual person who never gets noticed. People do notice me, then rush to pretend they didn't realize I was there to begin with. They make note of my existence, and then dismiss me as easily as they would a fly. To them I'm invisible, deaf, retarded...unworthy.

Clerks will ask my husband or my son what I'm shopping for. Waiters will look to someone else at the table for my order. One of the few times I'm specifically noted as being a Real Live Person without gross mental deficiencies is when I'm headed for the entrance to a building, and then people fall all over themselves to grab the door for me.

That last thing is not a bad thing, by the way. I do appreciate it.

Who'd have thought the key to whipping up a little common courtesy would be for someone to break their back? Men and teen-aged boys will sprint across a parking lot to get to the door first so that they can open it. Little boys will shout WAIT! and expect you to remain still until they can come rescue you from the weight of the mall door.

After that, you go back to being pretty much invisible again, but what the hell. They've done their good deed for the day, you don't have to try to fight a heavy door from a seated position, and you both feel good, even if it's just for four seconds.

Some people go days on end without enjoying four seconds of common courtesy; I rarely go a day.

~

My life is divided into points of Before and After. Before I broke my back (or perhaps before my back was broken; it's not like I deliberately did it myself, though that would have been a pretty ballsy way to get attention) my son used to dye his hair on a nearly weekly basis: bright red or bright blue, jet black or bleached blond. He wore his jeans slung halfway down his ass, which would have inspired many before-school arguments if not for the way-too-big shirts that covered up his displaying of the boxer shorts. He was a typical teen, doing the typical teen Look At Me But Not Too Hard things.

Then afterwards...not so much. His clothing began to fit, his hair remained a natural almost-but-not-quite blond, and I didn't worry about him sneezing and finding his jeans around his ankles. He kept his hair cut and his I'm-a-man-now-dammit-goatee neatly trimmed.

He didn't want the attention, not even the I'm So Out There You Have To Look Away attention. He preferred to be anonymous in the presence of The Chair.

Whether he realized it or not, he quickly grasped that people would walk past with glances averted when I'd roll through the mall or the grocery store. Somewhere in the back of his brain was the notion that this was attention on some level, and he didn't want to be a part of or add to it with his neon colored hair and rap-star-wannabe clothing choices. He wanted to fade into the background when he was with me.

That's not a complaint; it's not a bad thing. It was never that he wanted disassociate himself from me, but he didn't want to add to it. He was young when it happened, just shy of sixteen years old, but he understood it wasn't something I did to get people to look at me, or to get them to stop looking at me. I didn't do it for the Feel Sorry For Me factor. I didn't allow this to happen out of some warped need to fulfill some deep and weird psychological hypochondriacal fantasy.

It was just an accident.

For several weeks he wrapped himself in blame; I was driving on an icy highway, headed to town to pick up school supplies and the latest But-Everyone-Has-Them sneakers, size 13.5, when a car on the other side of the highway lost control, slid across the median, and slammed into me almost head on. Yet when the emotional ice and dust settled, he realized that it didn't happen because I was going somewhere because he *had* to have new Nikes. It happened because someone else was driving too fast for the conditions and lost control of their vehicle.

Once he'd had his Lightbulb Moment and I was out of the hospital, his concerns were singularly focused. *Does this mean we have to get one of those ugly assed vans?*

There are some things that are extremely important to a kid on the verge of getting his driver's license, and the mode of transportation is one of them.

And hell no, I was not driving a van. You can get a spiffy looking convertible equipped with hand controls.

Which meant he couldn't borrow it.

See, there are some perks.

But, I get stared at a lot. And it's just another ~~reason~~ excuse on my list of Why I Have Not Gone 'Home' In Fifteen Years.

My disabilities are one more thing for the post-visit table fodder. I know them; while they do feel for me they haven't confronted the realities of me being me now. They haven't really had to go through the anger of it; there's been no watching me take those steps from being pulled out of the wreck to agonizing over therapy to finally being okay with it.

Talking to them on the phone, I realize that it's out of their heads, and unless I specifically mention it, they've pretty much forgotten the whole thing happened. And I suspect that's intentional: don't deal with the pain; just pretend it's not there.

So I'd visit and leave, and as soon as I was gone:

"My carpet will never be the same. Did

you see what that *chair* did to it? I'm not sure all those ruts will ever come out."

"You think she doesn't exercise because she uses the chair as an excuse not to? That really isn't a reason to let yourself get fat."

"She spends fifteen years away and could only give us a few days? It's not like she has a *job* she has to get back for."

"All those pills she takes...that has to be for show. She's not in that much pain. No one can be in that much pain and still be conscious."

"All Sam needs is six months with Jenny Craig and a good personal trainer."

Deep down, their hearts would probably be breaking for me, simply because they had never confronted the wheelchair. But eventually the gossip would erupt like one giant, vindictive boil, and by the end it wouldn't be Oh Poor Sam She's In A Wheelchair. It would be Why The Hell Did She Get So Fat?

I'd rather they stared.

3.

There aren't any valid reasons typed out in sharp bullet points, no lines highlighted in bright yellow, about why I haven't gone back to see my family in fifteen years. I do have a ton of excuses; those pour out easily and frequently. It's like water droplets on melting icicle; one breaks free and two more are there, ready to drip and form a icy little puddle.

In spite of the distance of a decade and a half and thousands of yes-I-miss-you-too phone calls I honestly feel no compulsion to get on a plane and visit, no matter how often they say they want me to. Their existence is a jumble of memory and factoids: half-way across the country I have elderly parents, two middle aged sisters, and a grown up nephew. There's also a brother-in-law whom I have never met, and his spastic little Chihuahua named Tornado that has a fondness for eating pillows, popcorn, and his own poop. Half of them live in a house I once called home and my room is still there waiting for me.

Still, I don't feel the need to plunk down a credit card to buy a plane ticket I'll spend the next six months paying for.

Then my son—who does visit his parents because they keep real food in the house and they don't squawk too loudly when half of it walks out the door with him—made cookies. He walked past my office and mentioned casually that there were fresh cookies in the kitchen and I was out of flour and eggs, and would it be all right to borrow the last of the milk?

Cookies. Warm, gooey, chocolate chip cookies. Confectionary crack. I rolled towards the kitchen, my brain watering when my mouth was only contemplating the first bite, and saw them on the cooling rack. And it hit me. Cookies are excuse number one.

Eight years old; half an hour before bedtime I went into the kitchen to get a snack, and the counters were covered with flattened brown paper grocery bags topped with chocolate chip cookies. That was nothing new; my mother made them every two weeks because they were my dad's only sweet-tooth weakness. He loved cookies and beer, and often together, though he did draw the line at actually dunking his cookies into the beer.

There were *a lot* of cookies this time, but I didn't think anything about it. It was cookies, dammit! No eight year old kid contemplates the Why of ten times the usual amount of baked chocolaty goodness. I grabbed three and sat down at the table to eat them.

I was biting into the second one when my mother came in. She stopped in her tracks, her eyes narrowed and she seethed, *What the hell do you think you're doing? Who said you could have those cookies?*

I couldn't get an answer out before she demanded to know how many I'd had.

Two. I could barely get it out as dropped the cookie to the table.

Who said you could have any? I know you didn't ask ME. Those cookies are for the boys' basketball team, not you.

My oldest sister had spent all afternoon baking them. She had them counted out exactly, and because I was so goddamned selfish, such a *pig*, three boys on the team weren't going to get a cookie. She wouldn't let me put the third one back. I'd touched it, it was now crawling with my eight year old cooties, so she made me chew through a haze of shame and swallow past the lump in my throat.

I spent the next half hour puking my guts out, and once I was in bed I spent a good hour crying with a pillow clamped over my face so no one would hear.

I was eight years old.

I'd eaten a couple of cookies, but I'd been fed a load of crap.

There had to have been 200 cookies covering the kitchen counters. There were at most twenty boys on the basketball team. My sister probably never realized three of the cookies were missing, and if she had, she wouldn't have cared. If she'd been home, she would have told me before I even saw them cooling in the kitchen that I could have a few if I wanted.

My mother went from normal to raging lunatic in less than 1.5 seconds, and I wound up feeling selfish and worthless and unworthy.

Over cookies.

Cookies Destroy Stereotypical Suburban Family.

Film at 11.

Oh, I want the phone calls and I want to know how they are doing and what they're up to, but I don't feel pressed to go see for myself.

Or maybe it's that I can't bring myself to.

Either way, to them I'm frozen at thirty, still on my feet, still walking away.

4.

The nosy little snoop in me often thought about peeking into neighbors' windows. Did they sit around the table for no apparent reason and just talk? Kill off a good two or three hours swapping stories about their day, sharing popcorn and sodas and stupid stories about who was doing what to whom in their little groups of friends? Did they cough up bits of gossip in tiny sprays of spit, laughing about the marginally idiotic things they had heard and seen, offering opinions on the grossly insane people with whom they had crossed paths? Did they discuss the homeless and what we could do for them? Did they weep for the less fortunate and make fun of those for whom conspicuous consumption is a sport?

We did that a lot, at least without much commiseration over the poor and the hungry. Nearly every night my mother and sister Ev and I would plop down at the table and talk. And laugh. And gossip. The subject of our talking and laughing and gossiping was usually oldest sister Kel; we'd sit there almost every damned night and verbally rip her to shreds.

Anything she did was fodder for our conversational cannon. Her failed relationships. How she was raising her son. Why she did this, why she did that. Oh, we could solve all her problems and make her a much better person over a couple of cans of Coke and Dr. Pepper; we could figure out every aspect of her pathetic little life and we could turn it inside out and upside down.

While we dissected her every decision and turned her life into verbal confetti she was down the hall, asleep, after having dealt with her son—the dad was long out of the picture—and after having juggled work all day and school well into night.

She worked hard to get ahead; we spent hours trying to drag her back. If she got an A on an important test, we wondered if the time she had spent studying wouldn't have been time better spent with her little boy. If she caught a break at work and had a little time off, we'd chastise her behind her back for not using the time to study.

She couldn't win. We wouldn't let her.

Did I mention my mother was right there in the middle of it, egging us on?

In the years since, when I realized what we had been doing, it dawned on me that if she was willing to participate in the verbal slaughter of one of her kids, she was probably willing to do it to all of her kids.

I don't want to be the subject of the night time sit-at-the-table-and-gossip fest after I've gone.

All right, I'm sure I already am, simply by virtue of not having been there in so long. They know enough about my personal trials to have a field day with it, but the biggest target is that I'd be going back over seventy pounds heavier than I left. And while to my face they'd either say nothing or say something stupid—a platitude designed to make me feel better ("Oh Sam, you're not *that* fat. My third cousin twice removed on my mother's side was so fat her legs spilled over the sides of the lawn chair...right before the canvas gave way and the chair collapsed!") but would really only call attention to my size—after I left they'd be all over it.

I knew she'd gained weight but not that much; well sure she said how much but people exaggerate.

How can anyone eat enough to get that big? Oh, well, yeah, she's had major health issues that caused part of it, but you know half of it is Pop Tarts for breakfast, fast food for lunch, crap for dinner, and a giant plate of cookies at night.

Oh, and pie, you know Sam loves that chocolate pie with the chocolate crust and chocolate whipped topping. A person just doesn't gain that much weight without stuffing themselves silly. And it's a shame because you know if she lost the weight, she'd be so nice looking.

Oh yeah, they would say that. *If* I lost weight I'd be nice looking. All the while conveniently forgetting that when I was thin, it was "wear dresses and you'll look nice." Or "Wear makeup and you'll be pretty." Or "get a purse so you can at least look like a girl."

Or.

Or.

Or.

I know that I'm not Miss America, bearer of the neon white smile and just-so perky forward-facing boobs. God knows no one ever let me forget that fact growing up. No, I won't wear a dress; I think make-up is over rated and pantyhose is one of the most idiotic things ever invented. We have leg hair for a reason, people; I don't see some pressing need to shave it off. I'm not a girly-girl and I don't want to be. Total strangers get it, and they don't care. My husband gets it, my son gets it; I am who I am, and what I am is an overgrown tomboy stuffed into the body of a middle aged woman. Friends understand and like me anyway. But to my family...if I would just do this or just do that a *little bit more*, I'd be nice looking. I'd be *pretty*.

That be would another dinner table topic. Why doesn't Sam want to be pretty?

Doesn't she care what other people think when they see her, that they think she's, you know, (whispers) gay? Does she *want* people to mistake her for a man?

All right…that actually has happened. I get called "sir" a lot, or I did when I was thinner and a lot more fit. But no, I don't care. When it happens and people fall all over themselves to apologize, I brush it off. It doesn't matter. It can't be just because I favor jeans and sweatshirts, because I get it on the phone all the time, too.

I don't mind being the topic of discussion. If they're talking about me, they're at least thinking about me. It's that mental finger pointed at me, the judgment, I mind. The trash talk.

I often wonder if Kel knew about how we sat around the table and ripped her apart, and how she would feel if she knew. Hell no, I am not telling her. And that's not just because I feel so guilty over my part in it. I *do* feel guilty. But it would totally change her relationship with our mother, and knowing that my mother did it but never meant to be mean (really, I don't think she did) why would I do that? What good would it do to make her feel so bad?

My mother still has that table. I think when she and my dad are gone, that's the only thing I want. And when I get it, I'll burn the damn thing.

5.

"What," a drunken friend asked, "was the worst Christmas present you ever got?"

To be fair, we were all at least a little tipsy; the vodka slush was plentiful, and we sat in plastic chairs forming a semi-circle on the front lawn, white Christmas lights twinkling in the tree canopy above us.

Fine, it was July and the lights were more functional than festive—better to see the booze with—but watching lightning bugs swarm around the lights, the apparent disappointment over discovering those weren't other fire flies looking to get lucky, brought on speculation about really crappy Christmases.

My father did not shop. The procurement of birthday presents and Christmas gifts was Women's Work, and the purchasing of clothing for a husband was a Wifely Duty to be performed once or twice a year, when a suit needed to be replaced, or when underwear and socks became too hole-riddled to be comfortable.

His only exception was the occasional purchase for his youngest daughter, things he knew she wanted but was fully aware she would never otherwise get. Footballs. Baseball gloves. The skateboard that nearly caused World War Three to erupt right there in our living room.

My mother was the recipient of thirty two tons of really horrible things picked out by pre-teens lacking the frontal lobe development necessary to realize that most depression-era-babies grown to be moms do not wish to parade around in tie-dyed t-shirts and skin tight jeans, nor do they especially wish to be gifted with an electric can opener or new vacuum cleaner. By the time we were teenagers, the shopping we did in lieu of our father was no better, simply more expensive.

So she did all the shopping, while Dad was either working or sitting in his den reading the newspaper.

Christmas was her victory, or her fault, depending on the circumstances.

When I was eight years old, it was her fault.

Most definitely her fault.

Everyone could remember the really ugly hand knitted sweater from Aunt Ida or the gender bender Betsy Wetsy doll given to a ten year old boy by a sibling with a mean streak. What I remembered was Christmas when I was eight years old. My sisters got a TV, an electric typewriter, a record player. I got clothes.

We all got clothes, but that was *all* I got.

If I'd been sixteen, I probably would have been thrilled; and hell, at sixteen I could have returned anything I couldn't bear to wear. But I was eight and wanted a toy or two or ten. Hell yes, I was a typical greedy kid and we weren't poor by any stretch of the imagination, so it wasn't as if clothes were a necessity afforded only at Christmas and birthdays. But I got clothes, and they weren't even things I'd want to wear. They were things my mother was constantly on my back about wearing: dresses, frilly tops, tights. And they were *pink.*

Oh yeah, I was a tomboy. I despised dresses and she knew it; pink could whip me into an inexplicable frenzy of anger that made me want to put my fist through a wall. But she equally despised the idea that her little girl was going to school every day dressed like the ten year old boy down the street.

I watched as my sisters enjoyed their new things, and sat back bubbling in a well of Everyone Hates Me.

My mother hated me.

Santa hated me.

Whoever invented dresses should just DIE. He should be ganged up upon, strangled by those pink tights and pummeled with the fringed black patent leather shoes from Hell.

Later I was asked why I wasn't paying with my new stuff; I told her—in my eight year old, snotty, you hate me, I hate you, life SUCKS voice—that I didn't get anything *to* play with. You can't play with STUPID tights and STUPID dresses, and even if you could, who would want to?

Certainly not me. I was not STUPID.

She seemed surprised—how could Sam have not gotten any of the 150 toys on her I HAVE To Get This ~~Wish~~ Demand List—but that didn't change anything. All my brain could comprehend was that my sisters had all this cool stuff, and I had clothes that even an Act of Congress could not force me to wear.

Clothes, I decided then, were not acceptable gifts. Clothing was a parental responsibility, and the only time giving clothing as a gift was tolerable was if it had been requested. Like a football jersey. Or a purple hooded sweatshirt. Those were all right.

Dresses were just mean.

Two days after Christmas she came home from an afternoon of post-holiday Oh My God Look At The Sales shopping, and had bought me books and board games, and an FM radio that I did not have to allow my sisters to so much as blink at if I so chose.

She was trying; it should have erased the disappointment of Christmas, but I never forgot it, and deep down never exactly forgave her.

She's occasionally wondered if that was what cemented my Inner Tomboy, if that was the reason I never again allowed myself to be stuffed into anything frilly or remotely girly.

I never outgrew being a tomboy. I don't know why; I was always assured by others that when puberty hit that I'd somehow magically become this *girl* and I'd actually like things like dresses and makeup, I'd want to buy pretty shoes with purses to match. Puberty hit and...nothing. I still didn't want to wear a dress, the idea of makeup boggled me, the only shoes I wanted were athletic, and if it didn't fit into my pocket, I didn't carry it. There was no way I was carrying a purse.

I don't have anything against those things, and I actually understand their appeal, but it's just not me. I see a dress on the clothing store rack and think "Damn, that's nice!" but I'm not going to want to wear it. Me is jeans and a sweatshirt, with my keys in my front pocket and my wallet in the back. Me is short hair, no makeup. I've always been comfortable with it, even when no one else has been.

For a very short time in elementary school my mother tried making me wear dresses to school. I fought that so much that she tried another tactic: I came home for lunch every day, so I had to wear a dress in the morning, and could put pants on for the afternoon. I think the reality of laundry got to her, and eventually I won.

I was a kid who loved school, but was suddenly sick a lot, miraculously recovering at lunch time. Eventually she reached the point that as long as what I wore was clean and presentable, it was all right.

After all, she had the magic of puberty to look forward to.

I imagine she was very disappointed. And back then, if you weren't a girly-girl by age twelve, then you must surely be, you know, a (whisper) homo-sex-ual (whisper, whisper) queer. That was completely unacceptable by anyone my parent's age, and was barely becoming accepted among my own age group.

I know they worried about it. God forbid there should be a gay person in the family. Why, if anyone found out, we'd have to move, and then lock the girl in the basement until she either croaked or straightened out.

When I emerged from my teens still unchanged and very much not gay, I'm sure they were amazed. When I got married and had a son of my own, their amazement was painted with befuddlement. And I'm certain my parents are still waiting (hoping, praying) for me to get bonked over the head by the Girly Stick.

I've wondered a lot over the years why I am the way I am. It's not a worry, just a curiosity. Look at me and if you're crude you'll surely think "dyke." But I don't know why I'm hardwired to prefer jeans and sweatshirts and to despise dresses and frilly things. They're all okay with it now, but I think just once my family would like to see me in something they consider gender appropriate.

I hate to tell them, but it's not going to happen. The older I get, the less I care about what other people think, and when you consider that I didn't really care all that much to begin with...

No point to all this. It just is.

Christmas sucked when I was eight years old, and may be the foundation of Why Sam Became A Drag King.

6.

I was barely fifteen. I pulled off the teen-age cliché of sneaking out my bedroom window to go to a party; I met new friends at the end of the street, four giggling girls crammed into the back seat of a primer-gray, rusty Oldsmobile convertible. The reason I was risking my freedom for the next six months was behind the wheel; he patted the front passenger seat and with a grin said he'd reserved it just for me.

Mr. Wonderful was a senior; he was damned cute and old enough to know better, but young enough to think it didn't matter. Girls laughed at his lamest jokes and treated him like the proverbial BMOC. He could date anyone he wanted to, but he chose to drive a bunch of sophomores to a too-bad-summer's-over party, surely to become Remember That Time I Got Drunk And...? for half the people there. It was destined to be one of Those Memories, an Event to be spoken of in mortified whispers at the ten year reunion. *Dude...I still can't believe I did that, and NAKED to boot.*

It was a kegger; for most the first, for a few it was the last.

I wasn't a drinker, but I was the new kid in school and would have done almost anything to fit in. I had friends but not *friends*, and was still floundering, trying to get a feel for who would eventually matter to me, who would become that acquaintance I simply acknowledged in the cafeteria, and who I would walk clear around campus to avoid.

A party invite? Hell, yes, I'd be there.

Ask my parents? Hell, no, I would not.

I knew better; any mention of a party would be met with rolled eyes and heavy sighs peppered with "You don't know these kids. We don't know their parents. You're not going to the first *thing* that interests you just to look cool."

There would be no debate about the merits of adolescent social activities and no arguing on my part that they never knew the parents of my friends in Texas once I was older than twelve. I simply went to bed early, claiming it had been a long day and my brain was fried, and after half an hour or so I carefully slid the window open and hopped out.

I didn't bother with stuffing the bed full

of pillows to make it look as if I was there sleeping; I was fifteen and no one had bothered to check on me at night since I was seven or eight years old.

It was a loud party, kids spilling out the windows and all over the lawn, music blaring. Led Zeppelin and Cheap Trick bounced off the walls in bass thumping wonder, and there was no conversation that wasn't shouted to be heard. Mr. Wonderful wanted to dance; I wanted to dance. Mr. Wonderful wanted to go make out; I wanted to go make out.

But Mr. Wonderful didn't want to hear the word "no" and as much as it ripped from me, no one else heard.

He got what he wanted, and left. I hid in a corner of the kitchen until I thought I could move without throwing up, and then found another ride home.

By midnight I was in my own room, peeling off my clothes, wondering if anyone would notice if I crept down the hall and into the bathroom. I wanted a hot shower, as hot as I could stand it for as long as I could stand it, but I didn't want to try to explain why I was suddenly getting up to bathe.

Sweating so hard I was sticking to the sheets? My dad would turn the air conditioner on and we'd all freeze, and I'd hear about that misery for weeks. I threw up a little and got it on myself? My mother would be in my room tearing the sheets off my bed, and she would surely notice that not only had I not puked my dinner up, but the bed had not been slept in.

In the end I dropped into bed and tried to sleep, willing the pounding in my head and churning in my stomach to go away. Everything hurt, from my hair to my toes, and the feeling of bed sheets rubbed across my skin like sandpaper.

There was no sleeping, not that night, and not much sleep at all for weeks, until exhaustion ran over me like a tank.

Tell my parents? That wasn't even a remote option. Telling them would mean having to hear that I got what I deserved for sneaking out to a party I knew I would have been forbidden to attend. Telling them would mean feeling worse than I already did. Telling them meant taking on the blame. It would mean hearing that they thought it was a deserved consequence of doing something just about every teenager does at one time or another. There was no fucking way I was telling them anything.

I never told a soul.

Until now.

7.

I think I was three years old.

My mother was crying; I was sitting at the table with chocolate chip cookies and a plastic cup filled with milk, and Ev and Kel were glued to their seats across from me, wide eyed, trying hard to not so much as blink, lest they miss anything.

"She asked me to," Dad sighed.

I didn't understand what the big deal was. I picked a chocolate chip out of one of the cookies and smashed it between my fingers, then licked off the remains.

"She's a little girl," Mom sobbed. "Now she looks—"

"She still looks like a little girl," Dad insisted. "Dammit, she cries every morning when you brush her hair and she's begged you to cut it."

"She's not old enough to decide that!"

"Well, I am."

"You didn't have to get it cut so short!"

Dad reached over and ruffled my now very short hair. "This is what she wanted. She looked at pictures, pointed to the one she liked, and asked if her hair could look like that, so I had the girl cut it the way Sam requested."

Mom's agony seeped out in waves. "Her bangs. You were only supposed to have them cut her bangs and *trim* the rest."

Dad shrugged, and headed for the door. "It's not your hair, it's hers. She likes it. What else matters?"

"She's not your son, dammit!" Mom shouted after him. When he didn't turn around she looked at Kel and said, "Keep an eye on your sisters," before she stomped off to the bathroom, slamming the door behind her.

I was still mashing chocolate chips between my fingers.

Kel leaned forward a bit and said quietly, "I like your haircut, Sammy. I think it's cute."

"You look like a boy," Ev giggled.

"Don't say that! You'll hurt her feelings."

I dunked the other cookie into the milk. "I don't care if I look like a boy. Daddy says that now it won't hurt when Mommy brushes my hair and when she washes it I won't get shampoo in my eyes on account of it won't take so long to wash it, and if I promise to be good and not be a little monster about taking a bath and letting her wash it every day I can get it cut again before it gets long, and..."

"Take a breath, kiddo!" Kel laughed.

Ev was fingering her shoulder length hair. "Now I kind of wish mine was short, too," she admitted. "It hurts when I try to get the tangles out."

"Don't ask to get it cut right now," Kel told her. "Mom is really upset."

"Daddy said I could," I said.

"I know, and it's not your fault that Mommy is upset, okay?"

"She gave me cookies," I reasoned.

Ev frowned. "Yeah, what's up with that? *We* didn't get cookies."

Kel sighed hard and got up, bringing the plate of cookies to the table. "I think you and I are old enough to get our own cookies."

"So am I!" I said.

Kel's eyebrow went up. "You can have one more, but that's it. If you don't eat dinner tonight I'll probably be the one in trouble."

"I don't want another one. But I could get it myself if I wanted."

Kel didn't argue. She took a bite out of a cookie, and looked at my newly cut hair, trying to not smile.

Someone won that fight, but I'm not really sure who.

8.

Kel got, as it was whispered around me, "in trouble" when I was nine years old. Women around the country were burning their bras and protesting for equal rights and equal pay, and the people in my life tip-toed around semantics, as if at some point I would fail to notice the end result of what Kel's "trouble" really was.

This was the year I learned that boys are dirty, dirty things and we should never trust them. I also learned that if, in your innocence, you ask "Since she's marrying the boy she slept with, is she still a virgin?" that at least one parental unit will explode in a barely understandable diatribe, and you'll walk away with the idea that S-E-X is a four letter word. And that we should avoid boys at all costs.

Yeah, that worked.

Or maybe it did. Ev still lives at home— she's pushing fifty years old—and she's never seriously dated. For her high school graduation, when they paired up boys with girls to walk down the auditorium aisles, she had to borrow the boyfriend of a junior, because she couldn't figure out how to get a guy on her own.

She never had a boyfriend in high school.

No, she's not gay, she's just a bitch.

I say that with all the love and affection a sister can muster. But she is a bitch. And I suspect that's a big reason why she still lives with Mommy and Daddy, letting them provide a roof over her head and food in her stomach, while she fritters her pay away on crap she doesn't need.

But I digress.

Our eldest sister got knocked up during her junior year of high school. After many conferences with the boy's parents, during which I was required to stay in Ev's room with the TV blaring and not listen because I might hear the words "sex" and "pregnant," it was determined that these two teenagers would get married. He would join the Army, she would have the baby, and they'd all live happily ever after. Amen.

I don't think anyone ever asked them what *they* wanted. He was only sixteen; she was barely seventeen. He didn't want to join the Army, but join it he did. His father marched him to a recruiter and signed away his son's future, he went to basic training, and then came home—a run down duplex he'd never before set eyes on—to a wife he didn't really want and a kid that terrified him.

And yet they were all surprised when he was cheating on her by the time he was twenty. And they were all *really* surprised when they divorced before his twenty second birthday.

Gosh. Who would have seen that coming?

In spite of it all, my sister apparently had a parenting gene that popped open like a primed zit. By the time her marriage exploded her son was four years old, and even though she swam in the deep end of the pool of poverty for years after, she always seemed to be in tune with him, knew what to do and when to do it without having to ask for advice or getting information from streams of well meaning but poorly written magazine articles.

But I often wonder what her life would have been like if she hadn't been forced to get married. If she'd been allowed to decide what to do, give the kid up for adoption or keep him. What kind of life would they have had if she'd been allowed to raise him with help from the family, without the shotgun wedding.

My oldest sister constantly fought the

crush of the proverbial rock and hard place until she was in her early forties, when she finally found Mr. Right.

But...what if?

And not just What If for her, but for the rest of us as well. A lot of what I was taught about boys was a direct result of her getting pregnant. It was the "Men give love to get sex, women give sex to get love" crap, and by God I should not even *think* about S-E-X until he'd said I Do and had one hell of a ring on my finger.

Yeah, that didn't work so well. I learned a lot more from my friends.

And I'm sure if she'd been allowed to keep her baby without getting married, I'd be here now bitching about how my childhood was ripped out from under me by having to co-exist with the little rugrat.

I'm here bitching no matter what.

I'm very good at that, it seems.

9.

"Your sister," I was told, "needs to get her priorities straight".

Well, yeah, don't we all...? I was trying to concentrate on chemistry homework, but I sucked so much at the subject that any interruption was most welcome. If I bombed the next test, I had a ready made excuse. *I tried; I read all the material and did all the homework, but no one would leave me alone while I tried to make sense of it.* I was required to study at the kitchen table because, theoretically, there was nothing there to distract me, and by God one of us kids was going to college.

Being the youngest, that would be me.

Studying in the kitchen was my dad's decision, announced halfway through in my sophomore year. I was a reasonably good student, my grades were decent, so he decided that studying in the kitchen, where someone was always banging around, either cleaning or cooking or searching for a snack, would be much less distracting than studying in my room. At my desk. The desk that was purchased a year before so I would have a nice quiet place to study.

Parental logic at work.

I hadn't paid a lot of attention at the beginning of the semester (those dirty, dirty boys distracting me with their dirty, dirty presence, a cute one even seated *right next to me,*) so I missed the whole Avogadro's Number thing, and the Mole, and was hopelessly lost; disrupting me while I tried to make sense of the things to which I had not paid attention did not come without a sense of relief. If my mom wanted to discuss my sister's priorities, well surely that was more important than figuring out whatever the hell one studies in chemistry class (don't ask me, I don't remember, other than that Mole thingy, and the guy named Avogadro, whose number I still don't recall and wouldn't dial it if I did.)

My eldest sister had decided that she needed to go back to school. She was floundering (read: broke all the time) in her work as a clerk in an accounting office and she wanted to be more. She didn't want to just file away peoples' taxes, she wanted to understand them. She didn't want to make copies of spreadsheets, she wanted to create them. She wanted to be an accountant.

She wanted to feed her son something better than cheap generic pasta from a can three times a week; she didn't want him to grow up thinking that off-brand bologna counted as a meat serving. She wanted out of Section 8 housing and she craved safety for her son.

This meant that the rest of us would be expected to babysit. Initially my parents were all for it, until it dawned on my mother that meant her.

At that point in time my Ev had a job, too, and frequently worked until after 10 p.m. I often had homework; I could watch him while I did most of it, but sometimes I needed to give it my full attention. You just don't try to read *Oedipus Rex* while trying to explain to a six year old why he can't have fifteen Oreo cookies for snack or why Grandma's head will explode if we squirt an entire bottle of Hershey's syrup into the bag of potato chips, even if I kind of wanted to try that, too.

So this evening the topic was Why My Sister Is Selfish For Moving Back In And Trying To Further Her Education.

"Did she even think about how much that little boy would miss her while she's taking those classes? He sees her for all of an hour a day."

"She's looking for the payoff at the end," I supposed.

My mom sat at the table with me; I closed the textbook because I knew The Joy of Magnesium was no longer the subject at hand.

"But he needs her *now.*"

Translation: *I raised my kids already. I do not want to spend the next two years wrestling the little monster into the bathtub and into bed, I'm tired of cooking for them, I'm tired of cleaning for them, I'm tired, I'm tired, I'm tired...*

I couldn't really argue the point too much; we were all tired. If I'd been allowed to get a part time job—which I wasn't, because I needed to spend my free time sitting at the kitchen table, studying where there were no distractions—I would have been in school all day, then working, then taking care of my sister's son so that my mom could get off her feet for a bit.

"If she does this now, though," I pointed out, playing Devil's Advocate, "later she'll earn enough that she can be out on her own and they won't live with you anymore."

It occurred to me as that came out of my mouth that might be the real issue; she didn't want to raise her grandson but she also didn't want them to leave.

"She's putting all this time into becoming a glorified bookkeeper!"

"Accountants make a whole lot more money, don't they?" I shrugged. I was sure they did, but it was not my job to say so. My job was to get to where I agreed with her; Kelly was a selfish, selfish person for wanting more out of life than she could get by being a file clerk. It was a damned hardship on us all, having to watch her son, to make sure he had dinner and a bath and then a snack. Playing games with him and making sure he didn't watch too much TV was just hard work.

We were all martyrs to the cause.

"Just once I'd like her to consider our needs."

Like her needs were considered when she was pretty much forced to get married at seventeen. Or her needs when Don Juan walked out on her, finally, and it was demanded that she move home—to a place she'd never lived—for the good of her son. Or their needs when it was pointed out, less than three months later, that she could qualify for Section 8 housing.

Oh yeah, we were a family all about considering others' needs.

"I had to clean his bedroom today," my mother sighed. "I found *food* under your nephew's bed. He's been taking snacks into his room!"

Perish the thought. The boy should be dragged out of bed and spanked.

"I won't take food into my room anymore," I offered.

"Oh it's not you. You won't leave old bread or apples in there to rot. He was just too lazy to bring his plate back out so he shoved it under the bed. What was he thinking?"

He was six years old; I doubt he was thinking at all.

"Still," I pressed the issue, "if it's going to be a rule for one of us, it has to be a rule for all of us. We don't need to eat in our rooms."

She glanced towards the living room. "Well, that's not fair to your father. He likes to take a little snack into the den when he goes back there to read. I'll just have to keep an eye on the boy. But really, your sister needs to start thinking about the rest of us..."

Broken record, broken record, broken record...

10.

I'm almost forty five and I still don't know what I want to be when I grow up. I've had odd notions throughout my life, but I've never followed anything from the idea and the want to an accomplishment.

When I was ten I decided I wanted to be a writer. I wrote five page (double spaced) short stories and decided they were novels, and they were as awful as you'd imagine something being vomited from the mind of a ten year old. My most stellar piece was a story about a girl who decides to get married over her father's objections; he was so determined that she wouldn't engage in any matrimonial harmony that he kicked in the church door and mowed everyone down with a machine gun. I titled it *'Til Death Do Us Part* and I was sure it was the most extraordinary, incredible, mind-blowing, phenomenal, (thesaurus-riddled) concept ever put to paper. Surely no one else had ever thought of something that clever. It was amazing, my mind was amazing, my talent was *brilliantly* amazing.

I would win awards.

It would make me rich.

I held onto the idea of being a writer until I was thirteen. I scribbled out bad poetry and short stories, and sometime around eighth grade I decided to write something that really was book length.

And about my favorite subject.

Star Trek.

My wondrous tome had Captain Kirk, Mr. Spock, Dr. McCoy, the Yeoman, Nurse Chapel, and that one poor red-shirted security ensign crash landing on this planet where they were taken hostage and held captive in quite comfortable and lush surroundings for a very long time. And in my newly-hormone-drenched mind, there had to be romance. So of course Spock got it on with the nurse, and Kirk knocked up the Yeoman.

I let my mother read it; she laughed and snorted, "Well, *someone* has been daydreaming." My critic, she of the Harlequin-A-Day habit, as if daydreaming was a bad thing.

I know it was horrible stuff, but that's what you write when you're thirteen and awash in brand new hormones. Horrible stuff.

Sooner rather than later, I gave up on

the idea of becoming One with the New York Times Bestseller's List. I wanted to be a teacher. It was one of those things I let ferment in the back of my head for a few years. I loved school, I got along with my teachers; I wanted to join their ranks and warp little minds.

My junior year of high school, when we were being told in large groups of disinterested pools of acne, that we needed to focus on something that would determine where we would go to college, and in what we would major, that my Dad threw water over the teaching fire.

You can do much better than that, he said. You could run your own business. Hell, major in business, then come up with a good proposal, and I'll even invest in it.

At the time, it wasn't a "Screw him, I want to teach" kind of thing. It was "Damn! He thinks a lot of me. And he's smart...I should do this."

I shoved the idea of majoring in education aside, but after my first semester of college I realized there was no way I could survive getting a business degree without my eyeballs imploding in a mass of God I'm Bored. I hated the classes, and I gradually shifted towards becoming an English major.

You know, you really can't do a lot with an English degree.

I got married before I graduated, and stepped into a career of floundering, at which I've been very good. I've worked odd jobs, but for the most part, I raised my kid and saw my husband through grad school. And that's not a complaint. I loved being a mom, and I loved the stupid odd jobs I did, even when they didn't pay much.

But now my kid is grown, and I'm finding myself bored most of the time. I'm almost forty-freaking-five years old, and I think I need to know what it is I want to be when I finally grow up.

I know I haven't grown up, because I want something to just fall into my lap. I want the perfect job to come looking for me. I want career fulfillment, a paycheck, but I don't want to have to figure out how to get that. But if I did get it—you would never see someone work as hard.

I'm backwards that way.

Not grown up, and backwards.

11.

I wonder sometimes if parents stop and think before they name their kids. When my son was five he had a crush on a girl named LaCretia; she was cute and funny, and was the best player on their T-ball team, but it only took a few days for the kids to warp her name into La Creature.

There was another kid named Shannon; that in itself was no big deal, but Shannon was a six year old boy who was actually beat up a few times for having a girly name. Later Simon encountered an Ethel, who went through high school known as Grandma.

Before he was born we debated over the alliterative merits of Simon Stark; would kids make fun of it? Was there something we were missing in the bigger picture? Did it rhyme with anything embarrassing? Were we dooming him to a grade school life of being taunted with things like 'Simple Simon Stark and Stupid?'

We toyed with naming him after my brother, but it was too big of a Screw You to thrust at my parents. I had no idea how they would react and Scott wasn't ready to face them over anything, much less his son's name.

We settled on Simon Scott Stark, risking his lifelong issues over being turned into a limerick or two by the time he was ten.

I have issues with poorly chose names. I completely, wholly utterly despise my middle name. What were my parents thinking? Was there a debt owed? "Do this for me and I'll forget the fifty bucks you owe me." Was it grandmotherly pressure? "I *love* that name and if you don't use it I'll cut you out of my will!"

I'm fairly sure my parents could be bought on the cheap.

Eunice. Who names their kid Eunice? Was it ever popular? I don't recall meeting a single Eunice under the age of sixty, and I certainly never grew up with one in the same class or even the same school. It's not a family name; there are no pissed off Eunices hanging off even the high branches of the family tree. There are no distant-cousin-Eunices clinging to the roots. I doubt there were ever any close-friend Eunices for whom they wanted to name me.

I hate it with a passion that I normally reserve for things pink and for country music; I hear it and I want to put my foot through the closest stereo speaker. I cringe any time I'm required to divulge what my middle initial of "E" stands for; I'd rather be coated in honey and left standing naked in a field of fire ants.

So when in fourth grade, there were three girls named Samantha in the class, you can imagine how completely pissed off I was to have to answer to both my first and middle names.

Three girls named Samantha. Who'd have ever figured that? One swore she couldn't spell her own middle name, so she got to be Just Samantha. The other was Samantha Roberta and didn't mind being Just Middle Name. So I got stuck with being Samantha-Eunice. No, I was not allowed to be Sam or Sammy or even Sammi-with-an-i. God, people might think I was a BOY or something.

I cried about it at home. It was not fair; the other Samanthas didn't have to suffer the way I did. They did not have to live with the humiliation of a name that should only be spoken in whispers on someone's death bed. No one was ever going to want to be friends with the Worst Name Ever; it would be better if I just changed schools and got the trauma over with, because my life was OVER.

I was sure my mother would march to the school and inform my teacher that it was perfectly acceptable to call me Sam—everyone did, they had from Day One—and to stop torturing me. "Why, Miss Mulroony," she would say, "no one has ever mistaken Sam for a boy. We like calling her Sam. Call her Sam or I will pull your hair and make you cry!"

I begged her to intervene; she laughed, and told me to get over it. No one, she declared, was going to care that my middle name was Eunice.

My classmates might not have cared, but they all thought it was funny as hell, and made fourth grade a miserable, degrading experience. Kids would follow me down the hall sneering "Samantha *Yoooooonissss*" just because they knew it was a quick way to get a rise out of me, and the tears that often sprang to my eyes were a great source of humor. Kids would hoot at me as if I were a wayward owl, taunting me on the playground with "Yoo-hooo-hooo-hoooonissss!" In fourth grade, the battle cry of my name was sport, and I didn't want to play.

Yet I didn't blame them; even in fourth grade I knew they were doing what I would were I someone else. I blamed my mother for not having the guts to stand up for me and force the teacher into calling me Sam. Oh, I blamed the teacher, too, because she was a bitter old bitch who should not have been teaching little kids, and I hated her for inflicting her backwards notions on me.

(A year later the same teacher would stop me in the hallway to pronounce Kel to be a little whore who should be ashamed to show her face in town ever again. I was just enough of a smart ass to shoot back with "Why, just because she had sex and you never will?" I didn't have a clue what I was talking about, but it shut her up.)

So what if people thought Sam was a boy's name? Why would anyone really care?

I've considered changing my name...but who goes and changes their middle name only? I like my first name. I can be Samantha when I need to be, but most of the time I'm Just Sam, and I like that. Nothing personal to all the Eunices out there, but I hate it, hate it, hate it...yet I've left it alone. Figuring that one out might hurt what few brains cells I have left.

"You hate it and dwell on fourth grade," Linc once mused, his insight aided by a Long Island Ice Tea and a considerable amount of Mountain Dew laced with vodka, "because it still pisses you off that your parents would not march themselves down to the school to confront the offending teacher. Deep down, you wanted your mother to bitch slap Miss Mulrooney."

"I would pay to see that fight," Scott added, speaking to no one in particular.

"You should sue them for pain and suffering. The courts would surely back you up."

"And award you six dollars and thirteen cents," Scott snickered.

Scott does not liquor up well.

"I just want to know where they got the name, and why the hell don't Kel and Ev have sucky middle names?"

"Sam needs a new middle name," Linc told Scott. "We should anoint her with one."

"Eugenia," Scott offered. "So she can keep the initial."

"God, you're a dork."

"Ernestine." Linc offered.

"Estella."

"Very good!"

They clinked glasses together. "Success," Scott mumbled. "She shall be henceforth known as Samantha Eugestinella Camden Stark."

"It's beautiful," Linc sniffed.

"I hate you both."

"Now see how you are," Linc said. "We're trying to be helpful and you're just being mean. Why can't you be gracious and say 'thank you'?"

"Because," I sighed, taking a sip of my own drink, "my parents were evil people who saddled me with a crappy middle name, and I'm scarred for life."

Scott sucked in a deep breath. "You know, I once had a great, great aunt named Eunice."

Obviously, I let him live.

12.

Shortly after meeting Linc Farraday in seventh grade, the idea bubbled up somewhere in the back of my brain that my job in the game of Junior High Life was to torment him. No day would be complete without doing something to embarrass, humiliate, or generally pick on him. I sometimes spent the fifteen minutes of home room daydreaming ways to make him squirm, plotting what Evil I could inflict upon him without getting into too much trouble.

Locking him in the girls' bathroom.

Having him walk around school asking if anyone had seen Mike Hunt; the basketball coach wanted to see Mike Hunt in the boy's locker room.

Making him think he had misheard the history assignment; no, it wasn't read chapter six, page nine; it was read chapters six through nine, and answer all the review questions at the end of the chapters. At fifteen questions per chapter, he would surely have one hell of a night ahead.

Telling him on Friday after school let out that Monday was Superhero Day; everyone was supposed to dress like their favorite hero...and that he struck me as being the Batman type (made even better when he and his brother showed up in Batman and Superman costumes.)

Linc mistook my warped attention as friendly ribbing and didn't let it push him away. While I know deep down I was only trying to wring misery out of seventh grade for him, he asserts that I was the only one making an effort to include the new kid. Until I started picking on him, no one else would so much as fart in his general direction.

Obviously, my goal was to garner him friends through harassment, which was an acceptable enough for a kid who had just left the parochial school from Hell. Over the years I have tried to make him understand I thought he was a short, freckled little fly whose wings I only wanted rudely plucked, but he refuses to accept that I was not the nice kid he remembers.

This nice kid spent seventh grade making fun of Linc for the slip of an Irish accent that would pop out every now and then, for his odd home-haircut that always seemed in need of a comb; I invented reasons to make him the butt of a joke. While he was surviving his first semester in a public school, I was trying hard to fit in, too, and making fun of him helped me cement some of those pre-adolescent puzzle pieces into place.

By eighth grade my friends were allowing him to tag along; my personal objective was still the anti-care and continued torturing of Lincoln Farraday, but he had other friends who only occasionally wanted to wrap him in a wet blanket of humiliation. He was beginning to grow a bit of cool, the requisite fungus of thirteen year olds. Some kids had it, some didn't, and it could be wiped out by a single spray of Stupid.

Vincent Welch, the only sixteen year old in junior high, had a VW Bug. He also had the sense of humor one might expect from a sixteen year old perpetually stuck in 8th grade; after a Friday night basketball game, he agreed that loading as many people into his car as we could possibly manage sounded fun.

What else would a teenager whose best friends didn't even shave yet find amusing?

We piled kids in like logs, twisting and turning others to fill in the odd spaces, and then drove in wide circles around the parking lot.

I don't remember why it seemed like a good idea. No one was stoned. I think it just seemed funny. Arms and legs were sticking out the windows. Vincent was pushed up against the steering wheel and could barely breathe, but he managed to get the car started and moving.

It *was* funny until we heard the whoop of a siren and saw the flashing of red and blue lights. Bathed in the light of a cop's flashlight, we peeled ourselves out of the Bug one by one, until the unlucky SOB at the bottom of a fifteen kid pile—Linc, I made sure of it—flopped out.

What in the hell did we think we were doing?

At that moment, we were all staring at our shoes; most of us were probably trying to think of a way to explain it to our parents, while placing the blame squarely on someone else. And then Linc spoke up.

"We're testing Mitchum deodorant, sir."

Snickers. Laughter bit back with clenched jaws. Muffled giggles.

The light went to his face as everyone looked up. He stood there with thumbs hooked onto the pockets on his jeans, short and proud, grinning and not one bit afraid of the man with the gun. The cop stepped closer and sighed, "You're one of the Farraday kids, aren't you?"

"Yes, I am," he replied brightly.

The cop stepped back again, waving the light up and down the line of kids. "Go home," he said with a heavy sigh. "If his pop wasn't my shift leader..."

The threat trailed as he clicked the flashlight off and got back into his cruiser.

"Just so you know," Linc announced as everyone began to disperse, "*no one* here has working deodorant. Son of a bitch, you all stink."

That was about the time I realized that my own personal stink had nothing to do with body odor. I stunk as a friend, and the creepy little kid who was a quarter of a step short of being a stalker wasn't half bad. I still looked for ways to torment him, but the dynamics had shifted; I did make an effort to include him in everything after that.

Now he's eight inches taller than I am. He's quick witted and funny as hell, and he pays attention to small things. After I moved away, he was the only one making a concentrated effort to stay in touch. Other friends drifted away by the end of high school—and that's all right, because distance can and will do that, especially when you're so young. He never gave up, and he visits Steven's grave on all the important occasions, letting me know about the flowers that are placed just so, and the obvious dedication someone was placing in its care.

We've been friends for thirty three years; good friends for thirty two. I don't take that for granted very often, but I would send him on a search for a left handed smoke sifter in a heartbeat. And he would go, looking as long as he needed to, and one way or another he would find it for me.

13.

Steven met Linc in P.E. class. The gym was divided in half; one side for the boys, the other for the girls, and four classes met at the same time. There were days when the classes intermixed and we played each other in heated games of basketball or had relay races, and on days when the teachers felt particularly sadistic, we played dodge ball.

I hated dodge ball. It wasn't that I sucked at it so much as I hated the whole idea of it, picking some kid on the other side and pelting him with a red rubber ball that would leave welts as reminder of how much getting hit stung. I was never first out, but never last up, either.

Still, hating the game didn't keep me from strategizing with the others on my team; we wanted to win, and we'd pick our targets and take them out one by one.

And on this particular day, our target was Linc Farraday, the newest kid in our seventh grade class, one of the shortest kids in school and the least likely to survive beyond the third or fourth ball thrown in any given game; the team collectively decided that Linc would be the last standing on the other side of the gym. He would face a line of our best, and would run, screaming like a little girl, to avoid the pummeling that was sure to greet him.

We didn't want to hurt him; we only wanted to make him squeal, and quite possibly cry.

The problem? No one knew Steven all that well yet, and no one counted on him to not only figure out early on what we were doing, but on him protecting Linc. I was aware that Steven was fairly athletic, but I'd never really seen him in action. I didn't know he was light on his feet and quick, I had no idea he had good enough hand-eye coordination to slap one ball out of the air while reaching for another.

So Steven decided that he would be one of the last standing, along with Linc. And shortly towards the end of the game, Steven and Linc stopped throwing balls. They grabbed them, and set them on the floor until they had every last red rubber ball. It was just the two of them against eight or nine people from our side.

That was the day I learned that Steven could throw with deadly accuracy and a stinging speed that left everyone wanting more than anything for one of the teachers to blow a whistle and the game to be over.

The teachers watched with amusement; they knew what was happening and had no intention of removing us from what would surely be a Lesson Learned.

I was his first target, a screamer that pounced off my thigh and back to his side of the gym. Linc stood there, watching, letting Steven pick us off one by one. My team mates dodged and ran, shuffled from foot to foot and jumped, but my brand new brother showed no mercy, leaving welts and bruised egos to hobble off the floor to the bleachers.

"When you're the new kid you expect that kind of crap," Linc told me years later. He remembered the game as clearly as I did, and he knew that Steven had set out to make sure we didn't turn Linc into the giant joke we'd intended.

The thing was, no matter what we did to Linc, we couldn't hurt him. He'd spent the first years of his educational life in a parochial school and only left after being sucker punched in the face by a nun, for the crime of sticking his finger in his mouth during communion when he was choking on the Host. After the pain and humiliation of that, a bad game of dodge ball was not going to bother him.

It bothered Steven, who hissed at me

on the way out of the gym, "You don't pick on people just because you can. You play fair or you don't play."

I'd like to say that I had a personal epiphany that day, but truthfully, I thought he was being a pansy about the whole thing, and I said so.

Linc was a strange little kid, and strange little kids deserved to be picked on. It was the nature of the Junior High Beast, and the Beast must be fed.

How could Steven not see that?

14.

Eighth grade was the year of the Screaming Mrs. Zimmerman. She was three hundred years old, she was tired, and she didn't seem to care much for kids. Every seventh grader heard, every year, about the one teacher they did not want for English class in eighth grade, unless they wanted their every day to be turned into a sucking whine fest, with tears on a weekly basis.

You absolutely, positively, did not want to be assigned to Mrs. Zimmerman's class.

Those assigned to other teachers felt relief beyond comprehension, and made fun of the poor schmucks who were stuck with her for an hour every day.

Like me.

Some of them, however, while escaping the dreaded hour long I-Hate-You-Filthy-Kids class, wound up with her for fifteen minutes every morning for home room. It was fifteen minutes of Please God Don't Let

Her Look At Me Because Those Eyes Will Make My Head Explode In A Ball Of I-Hate-You Fire.

Every morning was the same: shuffle in, sit down and be quiet lest we awaken the beast slumbering within the elderly person standing near the chalk board, say "Here" upon the announcement of our own name, and then stand for the Pledge of Allegiance. By the time we were done, the bell would ring and off we would escape to a friendlier environment.

Until one day.

Several weeks into the school year came new kids. And these poor new kids were assigned to Mrs. Zimmerman's home room. They shuffled in, sat down and were quiet, said "here" when called upon, and then remained firmly in their seats when the rest of us stood to begin the Pledge.

Only half the kids had their hands over their hearts when Mrs. Zimmerman noticed, and demanded they get up.

No, they said. *We're not allowed. We're sorry*.

She sputtered. She turned three shades of red. Get off your damned butts *right now*.

No. Saying that pledge is against our religion.

I don't care. In my class you will get up and you will say the Pledge with your hand over your heart! This is not a communist country. We say the Pledge and honor the United States. Now get up!

No. We're only allowed to pledge an allegiance to God.

Get up!

We can't.

She yanked them both from their seats and dragged them from the room. Linc leaned towards me and whispered, "I think they must Pentecostal or something. They really *can't* say the pledge. It's like a mortal sin for them."

A few minutes later Mrs. Zimmerman was back, looking both smug and infuriated; we rushed through the Pledge and I'm sure a few desks were knocked over in the rush to get the hell away from her when the bell rang.

The next morning she was quite pleased with herself, pointing out that those "little commies" would not be back.

Halfway through roll call, her self satisfaction was snuffed out like a spit-upon candle. Linc Farraday's father, tailed by the vice principal, stormed into the classroom and without so much as a hello, started in on her.

He did not, he informed her, immigrate so that his son could be face to face with religious intolerance. He did not leave home and family so that the boy could be exposed to a mean spirited bigot on a daily basis. He would not tolerate her inflicting her sad little self and her narrow little views on any child, his or not. He would not allow his son to be a part of religious persecution. A teacher's job is to teach, not judge.

He motioned for Linc to get up. He would not allow his son to remain in her presence, and if he had anything to do with it, she would not be allowed near the rest of us for much longer.

For most of us, that was our first real civics lesson. And it stuck; we sought out the new kids. Is it true that you can't stand up and say the Pledge of Allegiance? Is Linc right, it's because of your religion? What did she do to you when she dragged you out of the class...?

Mrs. Zimmerman had a meltdown, and in the process those two kids made a class full of friends and fostered a need to champion the underdog and defend the picked upon in several students.

(All right, that particular need only lasted until the end of the semester, but the seeds were planted.)

Mr. Farraday didn't stop at pulling Linc out of her home room. He filed a complaint with the principal, then the school district, and when it seemed as if that would go nowhere, he mobilized angry parents to stand before the school board and demand answers.

It wasn't so much that they wanted her fired; they wanted her to stop screaming. They wanted her to publicly apologize to those kids. They wanted her to do her job and keep her personal rantings to herself. They just wanted her reigned in.

The more upset the parents were, the meaner Mrs. Zimmerman became. Do my job? Hell yes...ten page book report—due in three days. Pencil broke? Get out of my class and don't come back until you're prepared. Christmas vacation? Perfect time for a fifty page term paper. What, your glasses broke and you dare to utter the word Shit?

That lit the fuse on her internal ticking time bomb. When Rhonda Brickman broke her glasses and uttered the word "shit" under her breath, Mrs. Zimmerman slapped her.

The room went deadly quiet. Then someone up front uttered the Understatement of the Year—"You should *not* have done that"— as he closed his textbook with a bang. He got up, grabbed his stuff, and left. Then another left, and another...the class headed, en masse, to the principal's office. No one was going to let Mrs. Zimmerman get to him first. Yell at us, fine. Heap work on us, fine. But keep your hands off.

He heard Rhonda's version first, backed up by twenty witnesses. There wasn't a chance Mrs. Zimmerman would be able to deny anything.

Rhonda came to school the next day sporting a four fingered bruise on her face. She wanted Mrs. Zimmerman to see what she'd done; Rhonda wanted to make the old bag feel as guilty as she had been humiliated.

Mrs. Zimmerman was not there to bask in the consequences of her own anger. For home room we shuffled in and sat quietly for Mr. Browning, the vice principal. For English class we survived a string of substitute teachers. And for the rest of the year, Mr. Farraday and Mr. Brickman worked hard to make sure Mrs. Zimmerman would never grace another classroom.

I never saw her again, but I did see her obituary in the paper a couple of years later. I don't remember the cause of death but I will always remember "...preceded in death by her loving husband, and by her only son..."

Her son was thirteen years old when he died.

Mrs. Zimmerman was a bitter, lonely woman, and probably hated us for being alive when her own son was not. We were constant reminders that her son would never grow any older than we all were; she got to see us hit puberty and change, she was witness to our moments of happiness and sadness, and she would never see those things in her own child.

I didn't understand that, not even after reading the obituary. I was well into my twenties when it sunk in, during a conversation with Linc and his wife.

"Da," he said, "went a little bit nuts over the whole Pledge thing, but you have to keep in mind, just a year earlier I'd been punched in the face by a nun. He expected teachers in America to be open-minded and tolerant, and they weren't."

I'd forgotten about the punching nun whom Linc referred to as Sister Hubert Humphrey. In seventh grade he attended a parochial school; when she caught him trying to unstick the Host from the roof of his mouth, she punched him square in the face.

The next day, Linc was enrolled in public school.

The next year he suffered through Screaming Mrs. Zimmerman along with the rest of us, until his father intervened.

Linc's wife wondered if knowing about her son would have made a difference. No, we agreed, it wouldn't. She should not have been around kids, and even knowing she'd lost one, we would have hated her anyway. Linc's dad would have erupted regardless. Her pain didn't mean it was all right to inflict it on anyone else, especially not kids.

"But we can feel for her now," Linc added. "And say a prayer for her from time to time."

I've never said a prayer for Mrs. Zimmerman. I'm sure Linc has; that's just the kind of person he is. And in my middle age, I can certainly sympathize with her pain, but that doesn't change my memory of this old woman standing there screaming until her head damn near popped.

So maybe Linc is a better person than I, but I don't feel bad about it.

Maybe I should, but I don't.

15.

One of the things Steven always wanted as a kid but never got was a dog. His mother was allergic, and mine was phobic. He liked our cat, but there was always that want just under the surface. It had to be a real dog, though, not some spastic little hairless dog-wannabe. He wanted a German Shepherd, or a Black Lab. He wanted something that could eat a Rat Terrier for breakfast, but could be trained well enough to not inflict an early morning bloodbath on the family.

What he got with us was a cranky old cat that eyed him with suspicion and would slink away backwards at the sight of his size 11 shoes. Right around the time she relaxed and seemed to decide he was all right and would not purposely stomp on her tail with his giant feet, we moved and left him behind. She never seemed to realize that someone was missing, but I told him she would look for him every once in a while.

The family Steven moved in with had two kids of their own, but no pets. He had two surrogate older brothers that liked him well enough, surrogate parents that were happy to have him there, but he spent weeks feeling like a guest, not quite sure of his place within their family.

On his fifteenth birthday, Rob and Sharon Browning loaded the family into their station wagon; destination: Dinner Out To Celebrate Steven's Birthday. He got to pick the restaurant: Pizza Inn. Afterwards, he got to pick where they went for dessert: Dairy Queen. He was thrilled, and he thought that was it. And it was enough.

But the Brownings had other ideas. Through half a summer of Getting To Know You, Steven's surrogate brothers came to realize that what Steven needed was to *feel* needed, and to feel like a part of the family. And they figured out what he would most like to have in his life.

So instead of going home after ice cream, they had one more stop to make; friends of the elder Browning son had this girl they really wanted Steven to meet.

He groaned inwardly, but didn't protest. After all, if New Mom and New Dad and New Brothers wanted to play matchmaker once in a while, his life would not come to an abrupt halt. He knew how to be polite. He could make conversation; he was capable of making a girl feel important without committing to anything. So there was no rolling of the eyes or protesting "Hey, it's *my* birthday..."

The friend greeted them and told Steven he had the girl of his dreams. ("I thought he was insane, actually," Steven told me later. "I was fifteen; the girl of my dreams was actually kind of slutty.") He opened the door behind him, and out bounded a little reddish ball of fur with floppy ears and huge paws.

"Her name is Sasha, but she's young enough you can change that and she'll be fine."

She ran right to him, grabbing his pants leg between her teeth in a happy I-Choose-You tug.

Steven was in love. He didn't change her name; the musical lilt of Sasha felt perfect for the Golden Retriever that literally was the love of his life.

"That was when I felt like it was permanent," he said later. "I knew then that I wasn't going to wake up some morning to the news that they decided I'd be better off with my Dad again."

That's when I knew that someone loved my brother perhaps as much as I did.

Stupidly, I felt a bit jealous.

Wisely, I felt a lot of gratitude.

After Steven died, Linc told me, the

Brownings took Sasha to his grave at least twice a month. For the next seven years, he would frequently find either Sasha there with Rob or Sharon, or evidence that she had been there, the grass matted down where she rolled and scratched, offerings of a rawhide bone or a half destroyed chew toy.

When she died, the Brownings had her cremated and surreptitiously buried her remains in Steven's grave.

"It was freaky, really," Linc said. "Like she *knew* Steven was buried there, waiting for her. Yet at the same time she was damn near ecstatic, playing with her toys like he was on the other end of them playing back."

I expressed the proper amount of surprise—let's not make Linc think I believe in ghosts, after all—but the idea that Sasha could feel Steven when I couldn't filled me with a little glimmer of hope.

If she had a sense of his presence, maybe there really is something that comes after, and maybe it's all good.

Maybe there was hope for me after all.

16.

Eldest sister Kelly is in her early fifties now. Evelyn, the Other Sister, is just shy of fifty. Don't ask me exactly where in the fifties Kel happens to be, because I can never remember if she's six years older than I am or if she's seven, even though I can tell you for sure her birthday is two months to the day before mine. Don't ask me when Ev will turn fifty; I figure I'll know when I get an email from Kel snickering about our middle sister hitting the half century mark.

Our ages are a source of both amusement and pain for our mother. She finds Kel's graying hair and Ev crow's feet funny as hell until it dawns on her that she's a good thirty years older than her youngest child.

I'm determined to stay in my mid-forties, lest I get really, really old. I can't imagine myself really, really old, which actually ~~kind of~~ scares me. Most people seem to be able to muse about their senior years, the things they hope they'll do, the places they want to go and see when they're not encumbered with children and jobs; I can't imagine myself being that old, so it sometimes makes me wonder if I'll actually get to *be* old.

With the exception of Steven, family history suggests that I'll at least make it to my seventies. My father is into his eighties and my mother is getting there; all my grandparents managed to hang around well into their nineties, with the exception of Grandpa Theodore, who had the misfortune of being in a crosswalk when a sixteen year old driving his brand new Gremlin hit the gas instead of the brake and dragged him for a block and a half. He died at seventy eight, but I don't think that counts in terms of family longevity.

I refuse to count it.

I don't have a vision of my old age; I had a vision of my thirties and then forties, but that future-vision sort of stops at around fifty.

In my own mind I never really go gray. I never have the wrinkles of experience that will send me scurrying for huge shots of Botox. I don't slide out of middle age into my golden years; I just stop being.

"You're not going to suddenly croak the night before your fiftieth birthday," Scott assures me. "You don't see it because your friends seem to die in their fifties."

Linc raised eyebrows at that. "Dude, I am totally breaking up with you when I'm forty nine."

They're right; my friends don't seem to make it out of middle age.

Cases in point: Barbara Cohen, very close friend, the person who talked me through much of my post accident pain. She fell off a toilet, fracturing four vertebrae. While she laid in a hospital bed, her lupus and diabetes spiraled wildly out of control, and she was dead two weeks later.

Denise Coldwater, a friend who seemed to exist solely to argue with me about everything from politics to how much better my hair would look if I'd just put some highlights in it, died from breast cancer. Three months earlier she'd been told she was clear; she'd hit the five year mark and was "cured," but then we blinked and she was dead.

A third friend, Stephanie Corbin, so shy that she seemed stand-offish most of the time, lost her brother in the first WTC tower on 9/11; she never recovered from the heart ache and one day just dropped dead; even her doctor thought it was from a broken heart.

Okay, I hope that's why I have this lack of future vision, and not because there's some all-knowing voice in the back of my head urging me to make the most of things *now*, because now is all I have.

And yeah, I get that now is all anyone has. But I worry there's a finality to my Now that's in the not so distant future. And that worries me. There are things I haven't done that I want to, but that's not what bothers me. I want to live to see grandchildren, but that's not even what bothers me. What terrifies me is that I just haven't gotten myself right with God, and if I die hovering around fifty, I won't have done enough to make things right.

Sure, I believe in God. I believe in Heaven and all that. I don't believe in people being thrown into the pits of Hell for having lived flawed human lives, but I still worry. I've done some pretty stupid stuff in my life and I haven't made amends for it all and I'm not likely to. I fully admit I'm a sinner but I haven't gotten to the place where I'm willing to put myself out there and admit a lot of the sins, and engage in some real repentance.

Yes, I'm a coward. I think that makes me pretty human.

It also makes me very, very afraid of dying.

17.

Seventeen, my senior year of high school.

By then I had taken all the electives I needed, and only had two requisite classes to fill out the rest of the year. Like half the rest of those who would actually graduate, once fourth period was over and the bell signaling the start of lunch period was done ringing, I was in my car and headed for either fast food or home.

Most days I headed home instead of Scarf & Barf (think arches...golden, delicious arches with their golden, delicious fries) or any one of the other dozen or so places my friends might go (Scarf & Barf, Pay & Puke...we were clever with our renaming of the popular grease pits, in a we're-so-cool, dorky teenage way.) Lunch at home was free, and since I wasn't allowed to hold a job ("school is your job"), I had no paycheck to spend, and for whatever reason I couldn't fathom, I also was not given an allowance. If I wanted something, I had to ask for money; nine times out of ten it was deemed "You don't need that."

In rare moments of Understanding Your Teenager, my mother would hand me a five dollar bill, saying "just in case your friends go out after school tomorrow." I could milk that Abraham for a couple of weeks if I spaced out the times I hung with my friends, but those were few and far between.

So I went home for lunch. My free, make-it-yourself lunch, which usually consisted of a piece of cheese and a bunch of potato chips slapped between two slices of Wonder bread, and a Coke. Nutrition at its finest.

I almost always came home to the same thing: my mother and sister sitting at the kitchen table, flipping through magazines as they sipped their way through a seemingly endless supply of Coca Cola and Dr. Pepper. Once in a while, for a few weeks on end, Ev was employed and therefore not drinking her weight in soda every day, but I could count on her being there most of the time.

So. I was seventeen, and home for lunch. Mom was there, Ev was there, and Midnight the ancient cat was curled up on one of the empty chairs at the table, probably hoping for the spontaneous opening of cans of tuna or salmon. I shut the door behind me, dropped my books onto the table, reached into the fridge for a drink, and it started.

"Please tell me you didn't go to school dressed like that," my mother said as she quickly flipped her magazine shut, before I could see she was reading about sex. That was the pattern: Ev was on some dietary kick and was browsing women's magazines for all the latest and greatest ways to drop thirty pounds of ugly fat overnight without having to sweat, and Mom was trying to read about sex without anyone knowing she was reading about sex. She would talk about this recipe she'd just read, or that tidbit of celebrity gossip, but we all knew which pages of her monthly subscriptions were the most worn.

I took the bait. "Dressed how?"

"You look like a boy!"

"And the problem is...?"

Ev didn't look up from the wonders of the Ayds candy advertisement she was pondering. "I think the problem is that you look like a teenaged boy. Don't you care that your friends are probably laughing at you behind your back?"

"Then they're not exactly my friends, are they?"

Mom sighed, that little 'oh, come on' sound all mothers innately develop with the birth of their first child. "People can like you and still think you're...you know."

"Enlighten me." I damn well knew what she meant.

"Queer," Ev chimed in, a little too happily.

"That's such a nasty word." Mom fidgeted with her magazine. "You know, if your sister had cared more about what people think, she wouldn't be in the situation she's in right now."

"You mean *we* wouldn't be in the situation she's in right now," Ev offered.

I didn't see how what other people thought had anything to do with Kel's so-called situation but I let it go. "Speaking of whom, I can't babysit tonight."

"You have a date?" Mom asked hopefully.

Ev snickered, thumbing the pages on her magazine.

"Hey. You who are still a virgin. You're in no position to make fun of my love life, whatever it might be."

"You're not a—?" Mom's mouth dropped open.

"Holy hell. I'm going bowling. With *friends*. Yes, there will be male-type people there and yes I might happen to like one of them. But I'm not bonking him under the bleachers, and frankly, he doesn't think I look like a guy."

"Ah," Ev said. "He needs glasses."

"Shut up."

"Both of you, remember your sister," Mom cut in. "You don't want to turn out like that."

"Kel is a perfectly nice person," I pointed out.

"She's screwed up," Ev said.

"She's twenty four years old and she has a seven year old kid, a full time job, *and* she's going to school. She's *tired*."

Mom was shaking her head. "But she did some pretty bad things...I don't want either of you to make those mistakes. If she hadn't gotten mixed up with that boy, she would have gone to college right from high school, and she'd just be starting out, not starting over."

Our sister, Kelly; she of the Ooops Compulsory Marriage. Hell, *his* parents practically loaded the shotgun and pointed it at his back. All the adults agreed the union of two teenagers was a Very Good Thing, without much input from the kids involved.

When I was sixteen she was twenty three years old, and Don Juan—well, he was long gone. And somehow his stupidities were Kel's personal faults. He cheated on her, left her with no other warning, and it was her fault. She *must* have done something wrong, something other than try to make a life long commitment before she was old enough to fully understand that life does extend beyond age twenty one.

"Hey." Ev finally shoved the magazine aside. "Does this mean *I* have to babysit?"

"Would it kill you?"

Mom ignored me. "Just once you think your sister could find a real babysitter."

"When she said she wanted to take night classes you were all for it," I reminded her.

"But I didn't mean *every* night!"

"And I never agreed to babysit at all," Ev added.

That was true; we were volunteered. I never actually agreed to it, either, but there I was, night after night, playing Simon Says in the front yard with Tucker and his friends, or graciously losing to whatever board game he wanted to play.

(I liked it, there's no denying that; I routinely got to play, and Tucker was one of those kids that you just know is going to grow up to be a special case of Awesome. He was fun to be with and I still miss the creativity of his role playing games, where I was the alien from outer space, chasing him around the front yard with arms outstretched like a younger and trimmer Frankenstein. But still...I was not consulted.)

"I've done my child raising." Mom said. "I'm not—"

"Raising any more," I finished for her. "We know."

"I really have to babysit?"

"It's not fatal, Ev."

"Your sister should have thought of the rest of us before she decided to take classes every night. She never thinks about how what she does affects other people. You think she cares how much it costs us to keep a roof over their heads or food in her son?"

"I don't think she realizes it costs extra to feed them," Ev said.

I refrained from pointing out that the mortgage was the same, with or without Kel living there. And I didn't shove into Ev's face that she was as much of a moocher as anyone.

Ev was an unintentional moocher; if she'd considered that some day she'd be half a century old and still sitting at the kitchen table, things might have turned out differently for her.

One would hope, anyway.

"I sometimes wonder if she's even taking classes. I never see any books. Half the time I think she's out with her friends."

"What friends?" Ev snickered.

Mom's forehead crinkled under the weight of sudden consideration. "I never hear her talking about friends, either."

"They're hiding with her text books."

Kel was, and we all knew it, studying her ass off. She took her classes seriously, knowing that she might not ever have another opportunity like that.

Ev, on the other hand, barely graduated high school and never expressed an intention of going further. Her life consisted of talking about a job and watching soap operas. Every once in a while she would venture out into Real Life and work, but inevitably there would come the day when she'd walk through the door at night, humiliated because she'd been fired.

It was never her fault.

"I did *not* take money from the cash register. I just made a little mistake."

(Three thousand dollars of a little mistake.)

"I never called the customer an ugly son of a bitch."

(Not to his face, anyway.)

"They can't prove I used that pizza crust after I dropped it on the floor."

(Other than those five witnesses.)

Kel held a full time job that paid next to nothing, and spent her evenings in class. Ev worked sporadically here and there (though, admittedly, when Kel broached the subject about school, Ev was working full time and was not part of the How We'll Help Kel equation), wracking up credit card debt, and she spent her evenings sitting at the table, flipping through magazines and interrupting my homework.

Studying at the table was one of the few parental directives ever issued by my father, and only for me. I hit my sophomore year and he took a stand. *You will study, regardless of whether or not you actually have homework, for at least one hour every evening, and you will do it at the table where there is no TV or radio to distract you. You get good grades, and I want you to keep getting good grades.*

By God, one of his kids was going to college straight from high school.

I understood his intentions, but sharing the same space with Ev did not make for a distraction free zone. I'd get Tucker off to bed—which really only consisted of checking to see if he'd actually brushed his teeth and changed from his play clothes into clean underwear—then drag my books out, start my homework, and within ten minutes there she was. Given another fifteen or so and there Mom was. But I was at the table, books open, and that's what Dad saw.

It was educational, in its own way.

I learned to gossip. I learned to dish. I learned that in spite of myself, I loved to sit there and verbally destroy my sister, one muddled opinion at a time.

18.

I'm willing to bet, Steven tells me from time to time, *that if Kel knew about all those Round Table Discussions and how badly you still feel about them, she would forgive you.*

"Probably. She turned out to be the mature one, it seems."

So why do you let it gnaw on you?

"Oh, I don't know. Because it was so wrong? Because I was old enough then to know that you don't sit around and trash talk someone you're supposed to care about. Because I'm not sure I would be so forgiving."

Probably not.

"Bite me."

You know deep down that whatever you and Ev and your Mom were doing to Kel, they were probably doing the same thing to you.

"Were? I suspect they still are. But instead of pondering my sexual orientation, now they dish about why I won't visit, and

I'm sure they've invented excuses beyond anything I could cough up on my own."

They won't care about your weight, Sam.

"Like hell they won't. Only they won't say anything to my face, they would wait until I was gone. And there's the whole chair thing."

Now that they would care about, but not in the way you think.

"They know I can't walk, but they haven't had to deal with it up close and personal...Come on, you know how they would be. Somehow this would be my fault."

So you personally willed that car to slide over the median and hit you so hard your back just snapped. That's a talent you could take on the road, make a small fortune.

"They all know I'm not paralyzed. Somehow it would start with 'poor Sam' and become 'if she really wanted to, she could walk.'"

Could you?

"Telling you to go die in a fire right now would be redundant, wouldn't it?"

You have feeling in your legs. Why aren't you trying to use them?

"I did try. I tried for years. My back can't support me being on my feet for more than five seconds at a time."

So tell them that.

"I have told them that, but when it comes right down to it, that won't matter.

When they get to rolling on those little bitch fests..."

You haven't seen them in fifteen years. You don't know that they still do that.

"They do it on the phone. They do it in email. I don't want to do that anymore."

So you don't do it. You go see them, and when it starts, you just politely inform them that whoever is being dished about is someone you love, and you want to hear the good, not the gossip.

"That would require a backbone, and as you know, mine is broken."

They just want to see you, Sam.

"Yeah? How come none of them has ever wanted to come here? Why do I have to go there? It's a fucking two way route. Planes fly both directions."

They do.

"That's it? 'They do.' Where's your fountain of wisdom now, ghost boy?"

If I had any breath, I'd be wasting it. For whatever reason, you don't want to see them and nothing I say will make a difference.

"But I do want to see them."

You do, and yet you don't.

"Exactly."

How will you feel if your parents die, and you haven't gone back?

"I don't know."

That's just it, somewhere in that muddled brain you do know. And yet you still can't make yourself get on a plane and spend a weekend with them. Sooner or later you have to figure out why. And sooner would be better.

"Why do I talk to you?"

Because sometimes I'm the only sane one you've got, kiddo.

19.

Steven's NewMom and NewDad were either candidates for Most Understanding NewParents of the Decade, or Most Obtuse Guardians of the Century. While they gave him structure and rules—something he hadn't exactly had with my parents but was used to with his own mother—they also gave him considerable freedom, and that included allowing (or tolerating) him to visit me on a fairly frequent and predictable basis.

If they agreed to his travels, it was a giant leap of faith on their part; my parents never knew he was there and probably would not have welcomed him for even a few days at a time. Why disrupt the peace? With him out of sight, he was also out of mind, and they could pretend he didn't exist. If, in their minds, he was tucked away somewhat safely in a remote part of their little world, everything was fine and there was no reason to upset the metaphorical apple cart. But...we wanted to see each other, and since there was no way in hell I was ever going to be able to go there—I knew better than to even hint—the Brownings took chance after chance and allowed him to fly out to see me.

By the time he was sixteen he was well over six feet tall and sported more than peach fuzz; it was easy for him to rent a motel room with cash in hand. He relied on my friends and me for transportation and to their parents he was just another kid from school. None of them knew then that he was my brother, and the fact that he was with us sometimes and not with us other times rarely raised any questions, and when it did there were always viable excuses.

Aside from being a sometimes-member of the group I hung out with, he was my best friend Andrea's sometimes-boyfriend. When he was visiting, they spent a considerable amount of time together. When he went back home, they'd "had a fight" and weren't speaking. Her parents accepted it as teenage social turmoil, though after witnessing how many times people in our group paired up and then broke it off, it prompted her mother to mutter "I swear to God, you kids swap dates as often as most people change their underwear."

Either we dated within our own little group way too much, or Andrea's mother wasn't terribly hygienic.

After seven or eight visits in one year—
I never asked how Steven was able to afford
it, if he was ponying up the cash or if the
Brownings were, or if he often just snuck
out and came without permission—Steven
decided Andrea was better than a pretend
date. He had real feelings for her and the
only thing, aside from distance, complicat-
ing their growing relationship was a
girlfriend back home.

It was his less than honorable side. He
liked Andrea, but was supposedly half in love
with the girl back home. He drew careful
lines with Andrea, limits to what he would
do with her, but had none at home. Andrea
wanted more; Steven knew better. He could
date two girls at the same time, but he was
only going so far with one of them.

His reasoning: "I'm only here for a week
or two at a time, so how fair would that be?
She'd be waiting for me, and I sure as hell
wouldn't be waiting for her. As long as I don't
do *that*, it's not cheating."

He wanted her to feel free to date when
he wasn't there and wouldn't have been terribly upset to show up and have her involved
with someone and have no time or inclina-
tion to see him. Yet he had feelings for her.

I rolled my eyes a lot, too.

It was over after a year. They settled into
being good friends, swapping letters once a
week, sending cards for birthdays and

Christmas. She knew about his girlfriend back home, the girlfriend knew about Andrea. She seemed to be all right with the idea.

With a little prodding from Steven, they fostered their own friendship; she and Andrea began talking on the phone. If she needed to get a message to Steven, Andrea was who she called, knowing that a phone call to my house might be a mistake. If Steven was driving her nuts, she could always talk to Andrea. So when the junior prom rolled around and Andrea had no date, it was Steven's girlfriend who suggested he fly out and take her.

I didn't go to the prom. I was stuck at home playing Red Light Green Light and Sam Is Really An Alien in the front yard with Tucker and six of his friends. If I hadn't broken up with Boyfriend of the Month a couple of weeks before over something really stupid, I'd have been there. But no...my brother was at my prom and I wasn't.

Boyfriend of the Month, the little shit, found another date at the last minute. All that did was make me angrier. After all, he was the one who yelled at me for not being able to turn the steering wheel on his Piece-Of-Crap Celica as he tried to push it off the street and into the 7-11 parking lot. It's not my fault the damned thing didn't have power steering and that I just didn't have the strength...so when he got pissed off, I told him to shove it, jumped out of the car, and walked home.

Very mature, I was.

Andrea's parents were suitably impressed with her date. He picked her up in a borrowed car, took her to dinner and then the prom, and had her back by 1 a.m. There was no asking to stay out all night, no trying to convince them that the after-party at the Red Bird Inn was totally innocent. He came in to chat for a little bit, kissed her on the cheek, and left.

For a long time we all heard about how polite that Steven boy was, and why didn't he come around more?

Um, he works.

Ahhhhh...he has this HUGE test to study for.

Steven? He's volunteering at Mercy Hospital. Reading to kids...

I worried a bit when Andrea finally started dating someone else and Steven showed up in an unannounced visit. I expected questions to come flying out of her parents, but the square dance of dating squashed any curiosities they might have had. It was just another swapping of partners, and since the rest of us had managed to remain friends, there was no reason Steven and Andrea couldn't.

Then it seemed like an Of-Course kind

of thing. As a group, we dated and broke up, stayed friends, and dated someone else. Now it seems impressive, that they had that much maturity when they were seventeen years old. Had Steven lived, I think they would have been life-long friends. The rest of us...it's not like the group fractured; we simply went our separate ways, leaving for college, getting married, having kids. But those two would have stayed in touch.

His girlfriend back home—I think they broke up right after high school graduation. He was just shy of turning eighteen, and I often wonder if he would have done anything different if he'd known he only had two more years to live.

I wonder if we'd all have done things differently if we'd known.

20.

"I was in third grade," I said to Steven as he sat across the table from me; he fumbled with a can of Diet Coke from which he never took a sip. The moisture from the cold can condensed and dripped past his fingers onto the table, forming little pools that reflected only the ceiling above him. "The choir was part of the school's holiday performance, and we were required to wear white sweaters and dark colored skirts."

You wore a skirt?

"I had to. But that wasn't even the issue...I didn't own a white sweater. I told my mom at least a month ahead of time that I needed one, and then on the afternoon of the performance she erupted like this hormonal little volcano because I hadn't reminded her every day, twice a day. So I borrowed one from Kel."

Handy people, sisters.

"She had a white sweater and let me use

it, even though it was three sizes too big and more of an off-white than white-white. It technically fit the requirements, so I wore it, and I stood there proudly in the middle of the alto section, and sang my little heart out."

What, you didn't sing tenor back then?

"Shut up. That concert was supposed to be the highlight of the holidays. We'd practiced for two months and had it drummed into us how wonderful it was going to be and how proud our parents would feel. When it was over I was bubbling with excitement and just as jazzed as everyone else in the choir because we nailed every song. We sounded good, not like the herd of wounded hyenas we'd been afraid of sounding like. It had been as much fun as the teacher promised...all those parents were gushing, telling their kids how wonderful it was."

But...?

"But. I wormed my way through everyone to where my mom was sitting—Dad was not there, no big surprise—and the first thing she said to me was how embarrassed she was because in that sea of white, I looked dirty."

So the off-white did not go unnoticed.

"I looked dirty, the sweater looked dirty, everyone else looked so pretty, but then there was me, right in the middle sticking out like a ugly, dirty, ugly, sore, ugly, thumb."

Were you supposed to knit your own sweater?

"Who knows? It was made very clear that being the dirty looking little kid in the center of the choir was my fault, and now everyone would think she was this horrible mother for letting her daughter appear in public like that."

What'd she think about the performance?

"I doubt she heard the singing. When it comes to crap like that she has this target fixation; everything else fades into the background. She could be watching Jesus give a homily, and if there was a speck of grime on his brightly bleached robes, she'd be obsessing."

At least she was there. Not every important person in your life was.

"Dad didn't do kid's games and concerts. I never expected him to be there. But yeah, she was there...at least that's something."

21.

"I am so tired of watching Tucker." Mom squashed her spent cigarette into the ash-tray, and in one smooth movement was reaching for the pack to fish out another. "She's got at least another year before she finishes."

"More like three years," Ev helpfully pointed out. "She's studying under the Mo-lasses Method—one class at a time, slowly, slowly...."

My nose was buried in Shakespeare or Chaucer or some other dead English guy's work; since I wasn't going to be able to fo-cus it didn't really matter whether I was trying to memorize Willie's sonnets about the ugly broad or trying to read between the lines of *The Miller's Wife*.

When they first sat down, their talk was no more than a buzzing in the background, but as the subject tide turned towards Kel, they became animated, and I became distracted.

Ev was actually employed at this point, and I was involved in a school talent show; watching Tucker fell to our mother, who bore her burden with dramatic sighs and eye rolls, punctuated by the baking of cookies and pouring of milk.

No sense taking it out on him; he got cookies, we got an earful.

"Your father thinks she's starting to take advantage of us, that if she really wanted, she could afford an apartment and someone to babysit."

Translation: "I think she's taking advantage of me, and I want her to get an apartment and someone else to watch the little brat."

It took years, but I finally realized that all the things our father said were things our father never said. She simply didn't want to take responsibility for how she felt, and knew she could place the blame squarely on his shoulders. We'd never ask him about it; that would require initiating a conversation, something we avoided in case it turned into an hour long lesson on compound interest or the merits of fishing with a lure versus bait.

(Compound interest makes my head explode.)

(If you fish with bait, you can drink more beer.)

He's not the one who declared when I hit fourth grade that I had to wear dresses to school every day, forcing the issue until I felt nearly suicidal.

He's not the one who was embarrassed that his daughter was playing baseball in the afternoon with the boys from the street and thought I should seek out more female friends in the neighborhood, in spite of their nonexistence.

He's not the one who hired the kid down the street to cut the grass because that was not a girl's job, and I had no business handling a lawn mower, earning a little money of my own.

He's not the one who declared it was unthinkable for a girl to take auto shop in high school so she could learn how to take care of her car. That's what boyfriends were for.

He is, however, the one upon whom blame was heaped for all those thoughts.

"Kel makes more than minimum wage, you know," Ev added, again to be helpful. "And she has a full time job."

"So do you," I mumbled.

"I make five cents over minimum!"

Kel made about ten cents over minimum, which was all of about $2.35 an hour.

"Rent, food, utilities, car payment, insurance, gas, clothing, and child care, all on ten cents over minimum wage. Yeah, that'll work."

"It would if she were frugal," Ev snorted.

"And you're just the Queen of Frugal."

"The point," Mom inserted, "is that I am tired."

And she was. I didn't doubt that. While I wasn't witness to how she accomplished it, the house was always spotless, every single one of us had clean clothes, dinner was on the table every evening at 5:45, fifteen minutes after Dad got home, and if there was no one else to do it, dishes were washed and put away before she went to bed. She was at the age when she had expected to not be doing all that plus taking care of a small, extremely active little boy.

I was at the age where I expected to be concentrating on school, hanging out with my friends, and having fun; I didn't expect I would spend my afternoons studying and then babysitting all night.

We all resented it, but it wasn't Kel's fault.

"Couldn't you hire a babysitter a couple of afternoons a week so you could catch a break?" I wondered.

Mom snatched the cigarette from between her lips, angrily stabbing it into the ashtray. "I don't want Tucker to think I don't want him."

"But if Kel paid…"

"That would be different. He would know it's because she has to go to school, not because he's not wanted."

"He might have fun," Ev ventured. "If he went someplace for a couple hours a day where he could swim and play with other kids..."

"I will not pay someone else to watch my grandson!"

Ever a martyr to the cause; Kel was a horrible, horrible person for needing help, but God forbid anyone else's cash go to a babysitter.

I dropped out of the talent show.

I watched Tucker.

I resented the hell out of it, and like an ass, it was Kel I was pissed off with.

I was intelligent; I never said I was smart.

22.

Simon doesn't have to know about me. I was really just a blip of the radar of life; what good would it do to tell him now? It wouldn't just color how he sees his grandparents—it would color how he sees you.

"I'm not sure I deserve to be seen any other way."

So what will you tell him? That the grandparents he barely remembers, people he already thinks are a little off kilter, kicked one of their kids out and left him behind?

"Well…they did."

But that makes it sound a lot worse than it really was. You know how I felt about it. You know how much better off I was.

"I think I would tell him that he had an uncle, and I miss him very much."

You miss him so much that you've never mentioned his existence.

"I miss him so much that it hurts to talk about him."

Is that a reason, or just an excuse?

"It's very much a reason. I hate that Simon will never know you. I hate that he could have had a very different view of his extended family. I hate that he's so much like you without having had the chance to just hang out and be stupid with you."

Those who go before live on in the memories of those left behind—

"Yeah, I got that memo. I hate cutesy little platitudes."

—and they live more vividly when those memories are shared.

"You hate being stuck inside my brain cells."

I'm not exactly in a place to hate or not hate anything. I just am.

"Your mom should have had other kids. A lot of other kids...I dunno."

If she had, you probably never would have known I existed. If she'd had other kids, that might have meant a husband in her life, and a resident father figure for me. Would it be easier for you if I'd never existed?

"Easier, maybe, but not half as much fun."

We did create some fun, didn't we?

"Some. But I also wonder if some heartache could have been avoided if you hadn't been left behind."

Like a party you wouldn't have gone to if I had been there to stop you?

"Like a party you probably would have gone to *with* me. You never would have let me wander off with someone so much older. We probably would have gotten another ride there, and I wouldn't have been relying on someone I had no business trusting."

Or I would have refused to go, you would have gone anyway...me being there might not have changed anything.

"I can't help but think it would..."

I think the more likely scenario is that I would have been there, but I would have been very drunk. Probably too drunk to be much good to you.

"Even drunk you would have stopped me. Him."

I'd like to think I would have tried.

"That one thing...it's still a problem. It still touches everything I do, no matter how much I try to pretend it never happened. It's like this huge wall between Scott and me. We can peek over it but it's always there."

It probably bothers you more than it bothers him.

"Oh, come on. It's the elephant in the corner, only the elephant took a huge dump. You can't pretend it's not there."

No, but you can clean up after the elephant.

"There's no pooper scooper big enough."

Does Simon not know about that, either?

"Absolutely not."

Shouldn't he?

"What good would it do to tell him that? Why would I burden him with the image of that happening to his mother? Why put that into his head?"

So he could understand his mother better. So he knows why she has some shadows that occasionally frighten her.

"Everyone has those."

But not everyone hides them.

"Yeah, and I have little patience with people who fly their baggage like a personal little Look At Me flag. Get online sometime; it seems like there are more people whining than just talking there. So many people feel the pressing need to share all the little details…there are no boundaries."

Maybe they feel better once they've gotten it out.

"How? They share one thing, and then another, and another. It's like a never ending well of My Life Is Crap and they want the rest of the world to drink from it. My life isn't crap. I have a very good life."

So you tell him that. You tell him how good everything is, but there are these couple of things that happened, and those things made you a little skittish and shy.

"How about I just let him see how good life is, period. I'm sure he has his own crap to deal with."

And how can he ever deal with it, if no one has taught him how?

"No one taught *me* how."

Precisely.

23.

Ten years old.

There was a lengthy span of time when, as summer faded into fall, my mother would get sick. Coughing, hacking, headache, body aches. Cool fronts would move in, and she'd be miserable for days. It was exacerbated by her pack-and-a-half a day habit, lungs in protest over increased expectations, but she wouldn't quit, not for that.

Those long days of her misery made me feel powerless. Mothers are supposed to be the caregivers, not the ones curled up in a chair wrapped in a blanket, spewing forth gobs of gook hacked into flimsy tissues. Moms watch over sick kids, they don't get sick. And when they do take care of sick kids, they sometimes bring them little things that might make them feel a little better.

Like coloring books and funky twisty straws that inject a little fun into drinking all the You Need Extra Fluids juices.

I knew she wouldn't want a coloring book. But she did love books. And she wouldn't want a twisty straw or even Hi-C to drink, but she loved chocolate covered cherries.

I wanted my mother to feel better, so I strained for an idea. And when the little light bulb went off over my head I took what birthday money I had left, got Ev and Kel to kick in a dollar each, and I rode my bike to the convenience store just a mile away. They had a rack of paperback books, and they had tons of candy, and it was somewhere I was allowed to go by myself.

After much indecision and walking up and down the aisles, suffering the choices and not knowing what book would be better than another, I spotted a copy of *Please Don't Eat The Daisies*. Perfect. She loved the movie; surely she would love the book. And they had boxes upon boxes of gooey white filled chocolate covered cherries.

Score.

I plunked down my $4.50 and rode home quite content in the thought that I was doing Something Nice. I would give her these presents; she would smile and thank me and would feel at least a tiny bit better. And I would reluctantly admit that Ev and Kel were a small part of it, because even though it was my idea, they did contribute.

She was wrapped up in a blanket when

I got home, sitting in her chair in the living room, coughing into a tissue. Her eyes were red, rimmed by dark circles, and she was slumped forward, fatigue swirling around her in a phlegmatic fog. She was swimming in misery and snot, and I was about to shine a little sunlight onto her day.

I smiled and handed her the bag, and said something momentous along the lines of "Here, I hope you feel better."

She took the bag and peered inside, and we were suddenly enveloped in ice so thick it would have sunk the Titanic and ten of its little boat friends. She squinted and looked at me with suspicion that I could actually feel.

Where did you get this?

Almost a whisper, I squeaked out, "Seven-Eleven."

Where the hell did you get money for this?

"I used my birthday money. And Ev and Kel gave me some money, too." No, I was not going to now say that it was all my idea. If I was going to crash and burn, I was taking my sisters with me. "We wanted you to feel better."

She grunted and set the bag on the floor next to her chair. I got the hell out of there before anything else could be said.

Years later it occurred to me that she'd probably thought I'd stolen the book and the candy. Yep, I was so bright that I would have shoplifted and then handed the goods over to my own mother.

I'm sure there was a receipt in the bag, but I don't suppose she was looking for that.

The next time I made an effort to make her feel better when she was sick I was sixteen and she was standing on the back patio, trying to sweep up wet leaves. The temperature was hovering at around forty; she was wrapped up in a too-thin sweater, and was coughing her fool head off.

I slid the back door open and told her to go inside and let me finish sweeping. I don't know why getting those leaves up was so important to her; they would have been there later, when it was not so wet and cold outside. She was going at them with tired determination, so I took the broom and ordered my own mother inside where it was warm.

There were no arguments; when I pointed out that I was more than thirty years younger and had more gumption to withstand the cold, she handed me the broom and sighed "Oh, God, thank you." While I finished sweeping and shoving the wet leaves into giant plastic bags, she sat at the table with a mug of tea, watching me through the glass door, and when I was done she had a mug of hot chocolate waiting for me.

"You're a good kid, Charlie Brown," she said as she set the mug on the table.

Maybe so, but I felt a twinge of guilt; she was supposed to be inside just relaxing, not fixing me hot chocolate.

No good deed goes unpunished, I suppose. Whoever said that first was spot on.

24.

"I was always where I said I'd be."

Well, after Kel's wonder years...I can see not wanting to make the parents freak out.

"I suppose that was part of it. All of Kel's crap is probably why Ev hardly ever went anywhere. Who wants to be the next person to turn the family inside out?"

That would be me, showing up out of nowhere.

"I don't think you had anything to do with it, really. You were a separate issue entirely. It's just that I went to where I said I was going, and if plans changed I always called and let someone know. That's the same reason I was never given a curfew. If I said I'd be home by eleven, I'd be home by eleven."

Except that one time.

"Except that one time. But I *was* where I said I'd be. I was at the Shakey's Pizza with a group of kids from school, and from there we went Christmas Caroling. They knew I was leaving my car in the Shakey's parking lot, and they knew I was at the mercy of someone else to bring me back to it."

But then you were late getting home...

"...and Dad went out looking for me. When he got home he declared my car was not where I said it would be, therefore I was lying. I was out doing No Good."

For all he knew, you were.

"But my car was exactly where I said it would be, he just went to the wrong damned pizza place. Did he see the first pizza place he happened upon and decided, well, my daughter is a lying little tramp?"

But you can understand a little parental freaking, can't you?

"When I got home they started in on me and I didn't have a chance to get a word in edgewise. There were fingers pointed at me and a lot of 'We're so disappointed in you, how could you behave so selfishly, you're going to turn out just like your sister, you're grounded.'"

But the next day you showed them where you had been, and he admitted he'd gone to the wrong place looking for you.

"But he never apologized. Neither of them ever apologized. I was a freaking half an hour late because I had no way to get back to my car and no way to call home, and all I got out of showing him where I'd been was a grunt."

No proof you were actually there, kiddo.

"So? I had a good track record! You give a kid the benefit of the doubt when they're proven themselves over and over."

One might think so.

"And I was still grounded."

You were still late.

"I had no curfew! How can you be late when you don't have an actual curfew? And how the hell can a parent expect a kid to have money for a pay phone when they aren't allowed to have a job, and don't get an allowance? It's not like we had cell phones back then."

Minor details.

"I've never been able to understand how they think."

But all of the crap you dealt with, that made you a better parent, don't you think? You knew what you didn't want to do.

"It made me an angry person...I think I'm still angry. I'm mad as hell, and I don't always know why."

Maybe you're mad because you didn't get to be as much of a teenage screw-up as everyone else gets to be. Your older sister mucked it up in such a major way that you didn't feel you had a right to it.

"Yeah, but Tucker turned out to be the biggest happy accident anyone could have...and it's not like I walked on eggshells."

Yes, but as the youngest, if someone was

going to get the parental shaft, it was going to be you.

"You got shafted a lot worse."

When I was there. Have you ever wondered why Simon is your only child?

"Another kid just didn't happen. It's not like we did anything to prevent it."

But you don't mind that he's the only one.

"No, not really."

You knew what being the youngest was like, and you didn't want to do that to a kid of your own. If Simon was all there was, no one was going to lack attention, and no one was going to be judged by what an older sibling did or did not do.

"Or maybe I'm just so selfish that I didn't want the work another kid would entail. Maybe I'm so self centered I want it to be about me, all the time."

I can believe that.

"Gee, thanks."

Everyone is self centered. The only perception a person can have is through their own eyes. There's nothing wrong with making choices that benefit you, as long as they don't hurt someone else. So you only had one kid, because deep down, that's all you wanted. No harm, no foul. You didn't want to be the one to short change a kid from a mother's attention, because you didn't have that attention to give. It's got nothing to do with being a live-in babysitter; you were never hardwired to

*parent more than one kid at a time. If Kelly
had more kids, you might have duct taped
them all in one massive kiddy pile and locked
them in a closet.*

"I sometimes wonder if Scott is as okay
with only having had one child as he claims."

He wanted more?

"One or two."

Any regrets?

"On having Simon? Hell, no. Though I
have to admit, and I'm ashamed to admit it,
that if he'd been a girl..."

You'd have had another.

"Probably. I never envisioned myself as
having girls. I never wanted girls. Anytime I
gave it more than passing thought, I wanted
a son."

*You'd have been just as thrilled if he'd
popped out female.*

"That's just it. I don't think I would have
been. And I'm afraid I would have treated a
daughter...well, not as nicely as I should."

Bullshit.

"I honestly don't know."

*All you could imagine was a boy because
you were such a tomboy. And you'd have
probably raised a little girl to be a tree climb-
ing, bat swinging, football loving little monkey.
Don't sell yourself short for not being able to
imagine feelings you never had.*

"I can't help how I feel."

Guilt is the well worn badge of parent-

hood. Do you ever wonder what Simon will be chewing on in twenty or thirty years?

"All the time. And all I can do is hope that he doesn't feel as angry and confused as I do."

Your job was never to raise yourself a future friend, you know.

"No, but my job wasn't to raise someone who would spend the rest of his life feeling...this."

25.

I've only seen my father cry once.

Three o'clock in the morning, I stumbled out of my room, startled and tingling in fear over the ringing phone that had jerked me from sleep. My gut told me why the phone had cut through the middle of the night; I pulled the blankets around me tighter, willing the truth to go away, but after a few minutes I was plodding down the hall towards the kitchen.

Maybe it was something else; maybe it was a wrong number or a crank call. Maybe someone from the office needed my dad for an emergency. Maybe.

I willed there to be a fire in his office, the building a total loss and the call to be poorly timed information about his new lack of employment.

All the way down the hall, I willed it to be anything other than I knew what it was.

My father was sitting at the table, tears

in his eyes, staring at the wall and not seeing me at all.

"The boy died."

That's what my mother told me. The boy died. My father's only son, all of twenty years old, was dead.

While he stared numbly ahead, she began to putter around the kitchen, pouring water into the coffee pot, opening and closing cupboard doors as she looked for cups and sugar.

I stood there, rooted in place, pulse pounding in my head, fear and sorrow dripping from my fingertips in bursts of static that popped with every breath I could force myself to take.

"Are you going?" she asked him as she set a cup on the table in front of him.

He nodded.

"All right then." She was reaching for the phone book before he could draw in a low, deep breath, and was making him a plane reservation before he could blink past the tears.

I wanted to go with him; I wanted to go say goodbye to my brother, I wanted to be there when he was buried. I wanted to stand up at his funeral and tell the world what a kind and funny person he was, how much he loved the people who didn't seem to be able to love him back, and how I knew he would forgive them all. I wanted to be alone with my father long enough to tell him that I loved Steven, too.

I knew it wasn't happening; I wasn't going anywhere except back to bed, where I curled up in the dark, crying as hard as I could without being heard.

Steven was buried five days later.

"Lots of people there," Linc told me later. "The chapel was packed. Your dad kind of hung to the back until Rob practically dragged him to sit with the family."

"I doubt he felt like he deserved to be there."

"Eh, well, they obviously didn't agree. And man, your dad looked bad, like someone had stuck a knife in him and twisted."

Someone might as well have. I'd known for months that Steven was sick and the outcome was not going to be good; our father had only known for a few weeks.

The knife was in his back, and I put it there. I could have—should have—told him what I knew, but at Steven's pleading, I didn't. He wanted to tell his father in his own way, on his own time table.

He thought he could beat it. Deep down I knew what he wanted to be able to say was that he'd had cancer, but everything was fine. As his hair fell out, and the weight dripped off of him in waves, he refused to admit that the outcome could be anything but good.

Someday I'm going to corrupt your kids, Sam. I'm hanging around just for that. Your oldest—I'm getting the kid tattooed at sixteen. Just wait.

Simon came home just before his seventeenth birthday with a tattoo on his upper arm, a bright red, white, and blue peace symbol rimmed with flames. I thought it was beautiful; Scott sucked in a deep breath and asked how he could have possibly talked anyone into doing that to him.

"I don't look sixteen," Simon reasoned. "The guy just did it."

Scott poked at the red skin around the fresh ink, warned Simon to keep it clean, and let it go.

"It was a nice service," Linc went on. "Even the dog was there. She peed on the dirt at the grave side. No kidding, she walked up next to the casket, squatted, and let go right there."

I had to laugh. Steven would have thought that was funny as hell.

I'm her territory, she's marking me forever.

No one in my family talked about him after that. My father was quiet for months, he lost weight, his hair exploded in waves of gray, but he never spoke about Steven and I never saw him cry again.

26.

For the first few minutes after the accident, I thought I was fine. I was trapped inside my car, hanging upside down and held in place only by the webbing of a seat belt, but nothing hurt. I didn't see blood, and I had this fleeting thought that the whole thing could have been a ride at an amusement park. It had all the necessary elements: a few seconds of sheer terror, speed, and a nice twist at the end, all without paying $50 for admission and waiting two hours in line.

Before I had my bearings—yes, I really am hanging upside down with the shattered windshield about three millimeters from my nose—there were people surrounding my car, on their knees in the ice and snow, peering inside, hoping to not see what they feared they would. I wanted out of the car and asked the young man at my window if he could help me undo the seat belt; he stretched out on the ground next to me, and said that Just In Case, it would be better for me to wait for the EMTs. You know what They always say about accidents, never move the victim, blah blah blah. Unless you're just too uncomfortable and you think it's making things worse, let's just hang out and talk for a bit.

Ha ha ha. Let's hang out.

He saw what I didn't: the front end of the car battered into the shape of an accordion, the wheels bent in inexplicable directions. The steering wheel cracked and pressing so hard into my abdomen that it might have pierced through flesh. The back of the seat cracked in half. The reality that my legs were probably shattered and mangled into floppy little useless husks of skin.

The other driver, I wanted to know.

She's out of her car and walking around. I think she wants to come over and make sure you're okay, but other people are making her stay back.

I won't bite.

Yeah, but the police might want to talk to her before you do. You know, just in case.

Justin Case is a busy man today.

Then it hit me. Pain shot at me from every angle, searing, blinding, and overwhelming. I apologized to the young blond at my window, just as I threw up.

I'm gonna die, I'm gonna die, I'm gonna die.

He reached in through the window, sliding his hand down my side, as far into the wreckage as he could. When he pulled his hand back out, he looked at it and said, "No blood. That's good...I think."

Neither of us mentioned internal bleeding.

He reached in with a handkerchief and wiped the vomit off my face. He never shuddered, never seemed grossed out by chunks of my morning bowl of oatmeal in my nose and dribbling down my forehead. He cleaned my face off, and tossed it aside.

I suddenly wanted to see Scott and Simon. Where the hell were they? Why was I out there in the middle of nowhere, alone? Why the hell was I in North Dakota anyway? Whose bright idea was it to have an air force base so freaking far from the city?

What happened?

A lady in a Blazer hit some ice and spun out. She slid right through the median and into your car. Just dumb luck.

Is she drunk?

She doesn't seem to be, but she does seem to be freaking out over whether you're all right or not.

Tell her I am. Tell her—

The thought was interrupted by the sound of sirens blaring from down the highway; a speeding ambulance, a cop car, a racing fire truck. How could they be going so fast when the rest of us had to crawl along at twenty miles under the speed limit? What good would it do anyone if they flipped over, too?

God, don't let anyone *die* because I need help.

I could hear the crunching of tires behind my car, my poor, finally-paid-off little car.

What's your name? I asked the young man as he was getting up to make room for the EMTs.

Steven, he shouted back. *Be well.*

27.

Scott and I eloped; it wasn't because we had some strong impulse to get married right then and there—we'd been engaged for a year—but because when it came right down to it, I couldn't count on my family being there.

"Your father," my mother told me, "is against the whole idea. He thinks you're too young, and that you'll be pregnant within a year and ruin your entire future. He wants you to wait a few more years."

Wait for what? I wanted to know. He likes Scott. Yeah, we're young, so were you when you got married, and that seems to be holding together. We both came from families where you stay together through the thick and thin of it, because you've learned that eventually tides do turn and the proof is in the pudding, and every other clichéd, metaphorical thing that's ever been uttered.

Every step of the way, every thought about where the wedding would be held, who would be there, how big or how small or what sort of reception we wanted was met by parental resistance on a scale I'd never seen before. No one wanted to discuss it. No one would give an opinion or offer a helping hand, or even admit this was going to happen, no matter what.

We set a date, but it was met with shrugged shoulders. Apparently, by ignoring the fact of it, they could make it go away.

So early one December morning, we said to hell with them all—knowing Scott's parents would support whatever we decided to do—and headed for Nevada. By 10 a.m. we were married, and there wasn't a damned thing anyone could do about it.

My mother squealed in delight when I called to tell her. "I'm so happy for you!"

And at the moment, I believe she truly was. I was not offered the chance to speak with my father, and besides, what would be the point? To gloat? To say "The hell with you, old man, I did it anyway?"

Everyone was oh-so-happy. Sam got married. TO A MAN. If that didn't erase any of the doubts, what else would? It was suddenly Hurray For Sam. What a good wife she'll be. They're meant for each other; they'll be together forever and ever, amen, hallelujah and pass the pizza.

Yet none of them wanted to admit the marriage would happen, not until it did.

So we eloped. We pledged Forever in front of total strangers. No one we knew was watching with a smile or tears in their eyes. There was no organ churning out Here Comes The Bride. No throwing of the bouquet. No party afterwards for friends and family where wine and beer would flow and food would be consumed in massive thousand-calorie chunks. No rice or bird seed tossed into the air. No reception line where people would clumsily offer their congratulations while they eyed the open bar. There was no one except Scott, me, a witness from the county courthouse, and a justice of the peace who hinted strongly, with hand held out, that a minimal gratuity would be most welcome.

Scott slipped him a twenty dollar bill, which at the time might as well have been $200. We were college students living on ten cent boxes of generic macaroni and cheese; that much money would have fed us for two weeks.

A year later, those twenty dollars could have bought three and a half cans of baby formula.

So my father was right on one thing. Simon was born a little over a year later, just weeks before I graduated.

He's never gloated.

In fact, I'm not quite sure he's the one with all the objections. I never heard it from him. Not once. It all came from one source.

Your father thinks...

My ass.

28.

Ev was 21, and she was very drunk.

"He's married, married, married, married," she groaned, leaning her head back against the passenger seat of Mom's clunky station wagon. "She won't leave him, he won't leave her, all because of some damned kids."

"Staying together for the kids, what a concept."

"I see him every fricking day and every fricking day he's still wearing that fricking wedding ring like a fricking trophy, but he says he's so fricking miserable and just fricking wants out..."

Ev was not, as much as she hinted and intimated, sleeping with a married man from job #13. She wanted to; the fact that he was married was not a terrific hurdle for her to get over. He could stay married, she just wanted a boyfriend. And sex. And the occasional date, dinner out, maybe a movie. And sex. A late night phone call now and then, giggles and whispers. And sex.

She was getting none of that.

What she was getting was a reliable lunch companion who felt comfortable enough with her to share his misery. He talked about his lousy marriage, and she soaked it up as if she was a therapeutic sponge. She surely complained about her fruitcake family, and he was surely sympathetic. Somewhere along the line she decided she wanted more from him. Like sex.

"So tell him," I said, stopping at a red light, "what you want. Tell him you want to be the catalyst that will make his marriage implode. You want him to leave his kids behind for the Glory that is Ev."

"God, you're a bitch."

I did not deny it. *Samantha Camden, Super Bitch.* Able to leap small children in a single bound, unforgiving when someone tries to woo their (possibly temporarily) unhappy father away from their (possibly clueless)(and probably equally unhappy) mother.

"What the hell do you want? Either tell him or stop seeing him."

"I'm not actually *doing* anything."

"Bullshit."

"I'm not! It's just lunch. And talk. With possibilities."

"Find someone else to have lunch with,

Ev. Don't be the other woman, even if that's what he wants, too."

Ev didn't have to say it; there was no one else to have lunch with. The aroma of bitchiness wafted around her like a cloud of spilled perfume, and her other co-workers had long since given up trying to be nice. They all hated her, she was sure of it. She'd done nothing to deserve their antipathy, of course, but she was the target of it all the same.

The solution to her massive daily disappointment was to head to the nearest bar after her shift was over, and then to call home saying she'd gone out with friends and was now feeling a bit sick, so could someone come get her?

To produce further evidence of her ailment, she barfed in the car.

Two days later it was over. She never had to tell Mr. Commitment what she wanted. She never had to face trying to find someone else to talk to at lunch. Two days later she was fired, and she swore she had no idea why.

She found a customer's wallet on the floor near the cash register; she turned it in to her manager like a good little girl. She was surprised when the customer came to pick it up, and it was short three hundred dollars.

"I did not take money out of that

customer's wallet," she seethed. "Anyone could have taken the money."

True. Anyone could have. It was there on the floor, where other customers could have found it, where other employees could have seen it. It was there by the cash register—right in front of the security camera.

So Mr. Not-Right-Now was no longer an issue for her.

Mr. Not-Right-Now was the one who had fired her.

In a way, she was grateful, because who, after all, would want to be with a married guy who would cheat...?

29.

"You need to go home," Scott told me, as if the thought had never occurred to me.

Stubbornly, I retorted, "I *am* home."

"They're not getting any younger, Sam. Their health has been like crap the last few years, and it's not going to get any better."

"I know that."

"She *needs* to see you. So does your dad."

I started to answer but he shook his head.

"I know planes fly both ways, but they can't make the trip now and you know it. They're too old and too frail. Even Ev admits they're frail."

"And for all the years before now...?" I prompted.

"So? You didn't go see them for all those years, either. It just didn't happen, and there's no point in making an issue over who didn't go to see whom or why no one ever bothered to make the effort."

"When Simon was born, no one wanted to come out and see him. No one wanted to be here to help for a few days, other than your mother. She was practically here before you could get 'Sam wants you to come' out of your mouth."

He waited for the point.

"When Kel had Tucker my mom was on the first plane out. She was there before he was twenty four hours old. She stayed for two weeks and took a million freaking pictures, but when I needed her—"

"When Simon was born she had Tucker to care for."

"Bullshit. She watched him for two hours every afternoon, and my dad practically had to hold a gun to her head to get her to do that. Ev could have watched him for a few days. Hell, Tucker was eleven years old, old enough to practically watch himself; my dad could have taken a few days off to be at home in case Tucker needed help. But God Forbid he use any of his accumulated two years worth of vacation days so that someone could visit their brand new grandson."

"He wanted to cash them out when he retired."

"And a weeks' worth of vacation days weren't worth the birth of one of his grandkids."

Mr. I'll-Play-Devil's-Advocate—he agreed with me on principle—sighed, "So you won't go see them because of something that happened over twenty years ago?"

"God, Scott, it's so much more than that. When I had the accident, when no one knew if I would live or die, when I was plastered in an ICU bed without any idea if it was day or night, when we waited to find out if I would ever walk again—"

"—no one came then, either," he finished for me. "Yeah, I know. I've been pissed off about that, too."

"*Your* parents were glued to the hospital waiting room. The nurses told me they were praying out loud for me to be all right. Your dad *cried*. I never expected my Dad to want to come, I know better than that. But my Mom...she never had a problem with taking off to see my sister, or with going to see her own brothers and sisters for the hell of it. But she's never wanted to come see *me*, and I'm supposed to pee out sunshine because of it?"

"Sam."

"I'm her *daughter*, Scott. Why is it I have to go see her? Why is it she can't be bothered to come see me?"

"Because," he said simply. "Other than when Simon was born...you've never asked her to. It's as simple as that. You never asked."

30.

When Tucker was born, Kel was half-way across the country, living just outside an Army post in the middle of a military ghetto. Her husband was a brand new private and she was struggling with the change in culture, trying to muddle her way through the clash of her suburban middle class childhood with her almost-adult life of poverty level military dependency.

After months of complaining about the inconvenience Kel's teenage pregnancy had thrust upon the family, the headaches of the Essential Shotgun Wedding and getting the groom enlisted in the Army and through boot camp, Tucker's birth was celebrated as if he'd been the result of years of family planning and wished-upon coins tossed into the Fountain of Want.

The phone rang at six in the morning; after hanging up my mother ran down the hall squealing, "It's a boy! It's a boy!" and she began packing her bags right then. My father tried to roll over and go back to sleep, but she turned on all the lights and began tossing clothes across the room into her suitcase, jabbering on about getting to see her newborn grandson.

The embarrassment of his conception, the arguing over his parents' lack of wedded state, the mutterings of how much this was going to ruin everyone's lives vaporized the moment she knew her first grandchild was a healthy little boy, with lots of hair and a wicked case of infant acne.

She reveled in her grandmotherhood, calling every week to see how Kel and Tucker were doing; she willed herself to never miss a birthday and at Christmas baby Tucker found himself nearly drowned in a sea of Grandma's Gifts. Conversations with her friends were peppered with the details of his prodigal accomplishments: he was rolling over and reaching for things before he was three months old. He walked at ten months and spoke in clear sentences before he was fourteen months old. He learned to read by the time he was three and a half.

(Yes, he was a gifted child.)

(It runs in the family.)

(Simon.)

She was so focused on being a grandmother, even though the object of her obsession was nowhere around, that she wove her identity around it. She was no longer Ev and Sam's Mom, she was Tucker's Grandma.

Then Kel's marriage exploded in a mass of I'm In Love With Someone Else And I'm Leaving You. It was decided, in pretty much the same manner as her marriage—with very little of her input—that she would come home and start over...home being a place where she had never lived.

We left Steven behind, and brought Kel with us. We left Steven behind, and allowed Tucker to live with us. We left Steven behind, and filled what should have been his room with loud toys belonging to an even louder little boy, and the litter that small boys seem to generate simply by existing.

Kel didn't want to be there, but her heart was broken and she was still in shock; if there had been anywhere else she could have been, she would have been there.

Grandmotherhood lost its appeal for our mother. She loved the idea of her grandson, but only at a distance. She ached for the ideal of playing with him, getting him all riled up, and then sending him home, a home that was someplace other than hers.

I've already raised my kids was her mantra.

She was still muttering it on a daily basis when I left for college 3 years later.

I'm fairly certain she muttered it every

day for the next fifteen years, until Kel finally found Mr. Right and married him in a lavish ceremony that Mr. Right refused to allow anyone to ignore.

Hell, for all I know she still does it out of habit.

31.

Sometime between being cut out from my car—as I frantically searched the small crowd of onlookers for the Steven who had helped keep me calm as I waited for the EMTs—and being put into the ambulance, I passed out. I could feel it creeping up on me, a darkness seeping in like fog, electric sheets slipping over my head, tunnel vision squeezing my eyes; I fought against it, wanting to find him, to thank him, to get a good look at his face, his eyes, his smile.

It was just a guy named Steven, I told myself. *There are a million guys named Steven. It's coincidence. It's all just coincidence.*

I came to under bright lights with loud voices thundering around me; I wanted quiet but the air was filled with the static of frantic people shouting directions to one another, whispers of others asking questions in low hums that buzzed in the background.

"Is she allergic to anything?"

"Get a suture kit, I've got a nine year old with a deep laceration to his right forearm."

"Sam, can you hear me?"

"Sir, do you take any medications? Are you on aspirin or any blood thinners?"

"Sam."

"She's three years old, she's been throw-ing up since yesterday and now her fever is over a hundred and four. What's wrong with her?"

"Mrs. Stark, can you hear me? Open your eyes, Sam."

I think that's me.

My eyelids felt heavy and thick, and the world was a haze of blood red; I tried to open them, but it was easier to take a deep breath and whisper, "I can hear you."

"Can you open your eyes?"

"I can," I said thickly, "but I don't want to."

I heard someone snicker from several feet away, and felt a tingle of relief. If Simon was there, it couldn't be too bad. They wouldn't let a sixteen year old in the emer-gency room with his bloodied and vomit-covered mother if she was about to die—

—unless she really was about to die, and they wanted him to have a chance to say goodbye.

"She hates bright lights first thing in the

morning," I heard Simon say. "Shine it away from her face for a minute. If you don't, she'll just get bitchier."

That's my boy.

The blood red dimmed from my eyes, and I slowly opened them, squinting at the round, tired looking face looming over mine. "Where's Simon? Where's Scott?"

"Your son is right here, Sam. Your husband is on his way."

I turned my head, searching for Simon. "How bad—?"

Simon shrugged. "You've looked worse."

"It's freaking cold in here," I whined.

"You're naked," Simon snickered. "They cut your clothes off—"

"You were in a car accident, Sam," the doctor said, his face still hovering over mine, making me wish someone would offer him a giant tin of Altoids. "Do you remember any of it?"

"I was hanging upside down. I threw up all over myself and some young guy was there talking to me..."

"In the car?" Simon asked.

"No, someone who stopped to help. He just talked to me until help got there. Am I all right? Wait...why am I naked?"

"You have a blanket covering the gross parts," Simon assured me.

Dr. Altoid stood up and reached for my chart. "You're bruised up but we're most concerned about possible fractures in your spine, hips, and legs."

A grocery list of breakage. He read it off the chart in a very matter-of-fact voice. Milk, shattered ankles, eggs, broken back, bread, crushed knees, cheese, hip fractures, and M&Ms for dessert.

"Am I paralyzed?"

"You respond to stimulus, but we're waiting on a surgical consult—"

Simon stepped closer. "You're going to cut her open?"

Their voices became a drone in the background as I closed my eyes and I tried to drift past the noise. MRI. Cat scan. Broken vertebrae. Nerve damage. Metal rods. Hip fractures. Both legs broken. Damaged spleen.

Scott's voice. "What are the risks?"

Simon's voice. "Damn, it sounds like she might be better off if she *was* paralyzed."

Scott. "Will she be able to walk again?"

Simon. "Will she be in pain?"

Simon. "Will she be okay?"

Simon. "It's my fault. I asked her to go into town. She wouldn't have been there if I hadn't asked her to go."

Simon. "It's my fucking fault!"

Simon. "I'm sorry, Mom. I'm sorry. I'm sorry. I'm sorry."

32.

"Linc howled with laughter when he saw me. He couldn't believe I was going on a field trip dressed like a forty year old woman."

I was laughing, too, you know.

"I think I was the only one who wasn't laughing. Even Mr. Harlan was trying to bite his tongue. Like, what the hell? Who makes their thirteen year old dress in a pants suit four sizes too big just because they're 'representing' their school?"

Well, we both obviously know the answer.

"'You have to dress nice. You can't wear your regular school clothes, because they're not nice enough. You have to look like a girl.'"

Well of course. You were going to tour the Channel Four newsroom <u>and</u> the Dallas Morning News. Some reporter might see you and take your picture, and you'd be on the front page of the paper the next day. The headline would read: Samantha Camden, Eighth Grade Fashion Disaster.

"It was a freaking field trip!"

But you had to dress nicely; that was just one of the rules.

"I don't think I would have minded dressing nicely if it wasn't in her weird assed pants suit. How in the hell does something that big look *nice?*"

You think it was intentional?

"I don't know. I might even be able to respect intentional. At least then it would have been about me, you know?"

But it wasn't.

"It never is."

She sent you off looking like white trash trying to fit in with the socialites because she couldn't stand the idea that they'd all think you really were white trash...she didn't want people to think less of her as a mother.

"Think it worked? As if everyone didn't grasp on sight alone that there was no way I'd picked that outfit myself or chosen to wear it without a whole lot of crap being heaped on me."

We were all simply amused, Sam.

"And *you. You* got to wear jeans and sneakers!"

But I had on a very nice dress shirt. I looked quite spiffy.

"Did I really look like a scaled down forty year old woman?"

No, but I'm pretty sure that right now you're dressed like an overgrown preteen.

"And you're dressed like Goth Gone Bad."

Hey, I don't dress me. You dress me. If you don't like it, undress me.

"God, that sounds nasty."

I do what I can.

33.

I was eleven years old. Exactly.

There's a tradition in our family: on your birthday, you get to pick what the family has for dinner. The unspoken rule (which had not yet been shared with me) was that you always picked pizza. Italian sausage and green pepper, extra sauce, thin crust, sometimes with onion. Never pepperoni; I wasn't even aware of the existence of any variety of pizza toppings until I was in my teens.

Every year that I was old enough to voice my opinion, I picked pizza. It didn't matter if it was home made or if it was takeout, as long as it was pizza, all was right with the birthday world.

But when I turned eleven, I wanted hamburgers. On the grill. And french fries; those bake in the oven kind would have been fine. In fact, those would have been awesome. Unlike the fries my mom deep fried until they were 60% saturated oil, those had crinkles.

And there's nothing that says Happy Birthday like crinkle fries with ketchup.

"No one else wants burgers, Sam," I was told.

"But it's my birthday..." I had no other argument than that: it was my birthday and I wanted a freaking burger made on my dad's freaking grill, with ketchup and pickles, and freaking crinkle-cut frozen fries baked in the oven.

"Everyone else wants pizza."

"But..."

The matter was settled; they would all have take out pizza, and I would get a hamburger from Burger Buster.

I hated Burger Buster. And Buster Burger fries were soggy, greasy, and without a crinkle to be found on any of them.

An hour later she was home with two large pizzas, one burger, and one small fry. I peeled the wrapper back on my burger, thinking I'd just suck it up. A burger is a burger is a burger...

...unless it has lettuce and tomato and mustard and mayonnaise, with no pickles anywhere in site.

"This is gross," I declared, pushing it away from me. "It's got *stuff* on it."

My mom shrugged.

"Can I have a piece of pizza instead?"

I might as well have asked if I could have the keys to the car and money for gas to take my eleven year old self down to the nearest bar for a couple of Long Island Iced Teas.

"You asked for a burger, Sam. You got a burger. Now eat it."

"But..."

"No. The pizza is for your dad and your sister and me. If you wanted pizza you should have asked for it."

"I didn't want all this *stuff* on it." She knew that, too. Every hamburger she'd ever made for me had nothing but ketchup and pickles. "I'll throw up."

"I thought you might want a grown up's hamburger. And you won't throw up. Just eat it."

House rules. If you don't eat at least a little bit of your dinner, you get no dessert or snack later. But surely that didn't apply to birthday cake. On your own birthday.

I couldn't eat it. Not only was it disgusting, by then I was so upset I was choking on tears.

She brought out the cake—chocolate with chocolate frosting, my favorite—and they sang Happy Birthday to me, thin smiles pasted onto their faces. I blew out the candles, made a wish (probably for a slice or two of pizza) and my mom cut three slices.

One for Ev. One for my dad. One for her.

"You didn't eat dinner, Sam. Eat that burger and you can have a piece of cake."

The burger was in the trash can, I reminded her, and asked if I could make myself a sandwich instead.

No. Let it be a lesson. You get what you ask for, and if you don't like it, that's too bad.

Even on your birthday.

34.

I have this image in my head, ripped straight from a dozen TV shows and horrible, drippy, cavity-inducing movies. We're in my Dad's station wagon, pulling away as we head for our new home halfway across the country. I'm in the back seat—the rear one that faced the back of the car—waving at Steven as he stands on the curb, one arm folded protectively across his stomach, tears in his eyes, waving back.

But that never happened. When we left Texas for California, we left at five in the morning, when it was still dark and most of the neighborhood was fast asleep. Steven was across town, watching TV in a darkened room, pretending that life was normal and no one was being left behind. He'd lived in his new home for a month and seemed settled enough, though he felt like the other shoe was about to drop and he'd be jettisoned into yet another life.

I hadn't been able to argue on his behalf; there was no telling my parents what I thought about them, no threatening to run away if they didn't pull their heads out of their asses. Our father simply pulled Steven into his den one afternoon, told him the family was moving, but for his own good he was staying behind with the junior high vice principal.

"I hate them," I seethed later when Steven told me. "I hate them and hope they die."

"You do not."

"They're sending you to live with strangers. Who the hell does that?"

"They're not strangers, Sam, they're—"

I didn't care. "They might as well be," I snapped, cutting him off. "He's the vice principal! You'll never get away with anything again!"

"I'm not in junior high anymore, Einstein," Steven sighed.

"So? He'll collaborate with the high school principal. You know, 'Keep an eye on that Camden boy. I promised his parents he would never have any sort of fun at all while he lived with me.'"

That made Steven laugh. "You're so full of it."

"I'm pissed off."

"It'll be fine. I'm not living with strangers. I knew them before I knew you."

"But they're not family..."

"Sam."

"Family doesn't leave family behind!"

"Sam. Stop it. You don't know what you're talking about."

I didn't need to know. All I needed to know was that I was losing the brother I'd always wanted, and if I'd been given the choice, I probably would have stayed in Texas with him.

I certainly wasn't going to listen to him justify it.

All the way to California, as I dozed in the back of the station wagon, trying to ignore Ev's whining and our mother's Travel Guide persona as she pointed out the various sites to see—Look! There's a sign to go see The Big Mystery! Look! There's a sign that says Grand Canyon in two miles, but we're not going to stop for that even though the kids really want to!—I kept thinking of Steven standing there on the imaginary curb, waving frantically as his own father drove out of his life.

35.

The wheelchair the insurance company was willing to provide weighed over forty pounds and I couldn't get it in and out of the car by myself. It was too narrow for my ass to fit in comfortably, but it was cheap, it rolled, and therefore it was good enough for someone who was not, as was pointed out time after time, paralyzed.

"It's a temporary measure," one weary insurance underling told Scott over the phone, sounding as if he was reading from a script, hating the words he was forced to repeat. "There's no reason to get anything more than this because she won't need it for very long."

We did not share that optimism. My doctors certainly did not share it and battled on my behalf for a lightweight, easily maneuverable wheelchair.

We were almost amused; so much for free military medical care.

"We'll find a way to get you something better," Scott said often, and quietly in a voice that suggested he had no idea how; we were already deeply in debt from putting him through school and for Simon's orthodontia payments. We lived paycheck to paycheck on an Air Force Captain's salary; there should have been money to spend, but there wasn't.

"Two to three thousand dollars," I reminded him. "We have to replace my car...insurance isn't going to cover the full cost of a new one, and who knows how long it will be before we reach a settlement."

The Settlement. The dickering between lawyers over how much Sam's broken spine, shattered legs, and busted hips were worth. The woman who hit me fell all over herself in admitting guilt, but her insurance carrier only wanted to pay actual medical expenses. So what if I would spend the rest of my life trying to recover, both physically and mentally? You have military medical; it won't cost you a thing!

It might take years, we were warned. It doesn't matter what the woman who hit you wants for you; her hands are tied as much by her insurance company as you are by yours. Sue them now, don't wait until you're bankrupt. By the time you have cash in hand, you might very well be.

There was no way I was going to suck

any cash out of the little we could manage to scrape together to buy a lighter wheelchair. That was a convenience, I told Scott, not a necessity. I could live with waiting to go somewhere until either he or Simon could take me and be the muscle that gets the wheels out of the back seat.

Simon wanted to skip Christmas. "Save the money. I don't need anything. I don't *want* anything."

"Thanks, kiddo, but *we* want Christmas. You might not get a lot, but you'll get something."

"I don't need—"

"It's not about need," Scott told him. "It's about us wanting to celebrate."

"Celebrating shouldn't be about getting presents."

"Maybe not, but there we are. We're total Christmasites. Part of the fun we have is buying crap for you that will be shoved under the bed by New Years and given to Goodwill by July."

Simon grinned, the little boy in him peeking out just long enough to let us know that he wasn't entirely happy trying on his new adult attitude; he understood finances and pinching pennies, but deep down he hoped there really was a Santa Claus.

He would, we were determined, have a fairly normal holiday; we wanted to make up for practically blowing off Christmas the year before, when life was consumed with surgery and rehabilitation. We took a cash advance on Visa to pay MasterCard, and went shopping with the credit card payments. It would hurt later, but at that point we didn't care.

On a blustery cold December afternoon, almost a year after the accident, a UPS truck pulled into the driveway and the driver hauled out a hand truck to push the box he was delivering up the driveway.

Simon watched from the window, guessing that one or the other set of grandparents had sent gifts early. Likely Grandpa Stark, because he would want to drive Simon nuts for as long as possible, making him wonder what they'd sent.

I sent him outside to sign for the box, and he dragged it in through the kitchen to the living room, squinting to read the small print on the return address.

"Lincoln Farraday," he mumbled.

Surprised, I rolled over to him to look for myself. "What the hell is Linc up to now?"

"I don't know," Simon said, "but I think I'd stand about five feet back just in case it's full of those peanut can snakes."

He took a step back, partly in jest, but mostly serious. Linc was the giver of tongue-in-cheek gifts, from Superman Underoos for Simon's tenth birthday to snakes in a can on his twelfth to a stuffed Tickle Me Elmo for his fourteenth.

Anything could be in that box, and Simon wasn't so sure he wanted to be the one to open it.

"It's too big for me to handle," I said, just as wary. "Your testosterone wins you the honors."

He frowned, muttering that the box was addressed to me and not him, and someday I needed to be self sufficient and not rely on him for mundane tasks such as opening boxes from my psychotic friends.

In mid-complaint, after he'd opened the box, he looked into it with a squint and said quietly, "This is no joke."

"What?"

He pulled a slip of paper from the top and read it out loud. "'Once upon a time, I promised a friend that if a certain someone ever truly needed anything, I would take care of her in his place. You've always taken care of yourself and you've never really needed anything, but if he were here, he would want you to have this. I know he would.'

"I don't know who the friend is, but...it's a purple wheelchair."

"What? Seriously?"

"No, I'm lying. Because that would be *so* funny." He reached in and pulled the chair from the box with one hand. "Holy shit, this is light! Twenty pounds, tops."

I watched as he cut the ties that kept

the wheels from spinning and as he undid the brakes.

"There's another note," Simon said, pulling it off the seat. "'Don't tell me you can't accept this. If you do, Steven will dig his way out of his grave and come back to haunt you and eat your spicy brains.'"

There had been that momentary thought that I couldn't accept something so expensive from Linc, and I didn't know what Scott would say, but the image of Steven stomping towards me with zombie arms extended made me smile.

"Who's Steven?"

My breath caught, and for the slimmest of moments I considered telling him everything.

In a near whisper I told him, "Someone who loved me like a sister, a very long time ago. He was the uncle you never had, and someday when I can think about him without crying, I'll tell you about him."

He accepted it. He didn't press for anything more, but reached over to help me move from one chair to another.

"It fits," he said with a smile. "Like Linc knows how big your ass is."

"God, I owe him."

Simon shook his head. "I don't think you do. This is his Christmas, Mom. He gets off on doing things for other people. He wanted to be able to do this for you, and I doubt there are any strings attached. If anything at all, when you're more flush with cash, he would want you to help someone else out."

He was right. Pay it forward. That was Linc, and it would have been Steven.

36.

"How badly," I once asked Scott, "do you think we've screwed Simon up?"

Face it, other than Child Psychology 212 offered in your fifth semester of college as a social science elective, no one ever teaches you how to be a parent. You get horny, bonk like bunnies, and a few weeks later you're saying either "Yay!" or "Oops" when the little pee stick comes back with a plus sign on it, and then you BS your way through the next eighteen to twenty years.

You're bound to make a kid bleed every now and then while you improvise your way through potty training and little league, and you're surely going to piss them off on a daily basis through the wonder of the eye-rolling and huff-blowing teen angst years.

"Simon," Scott said, "will suck it up and get over anything stupid that we did."

I wasn't so sure. As I sat in my mental

corner every day, picking at old wounds and watching them ooze, I doubted I had a right to expect Simon to be anything but pissed off over our parental shortcomings.

"Every parent gets at least a hundred Stupid Passes," Scott argued. "He'll be fine."

Then why, I wondered, could I not give my parents a few of those passes? How could I expect Simon to be all forgiving when I couldn't whip up that tiny morsel of the Golden Rule in myself?

"Because we never hid a sibling from him," Scott said simply.

No, we just hid an uncle. How is that any better?

Linc's job had him crossing the country at least every other month; he hopped from military installation to military installation, carting documents in briefcases cuffed to his wrists, or escorting the less desirable military offenders to meet their judicial fate in hearings where the outcome was mostly decided before they even began. With Scott in the Air Force, that meant he often found his way to where ever we were stationed, and Simon saw enough of him to think of him as a surrogate uncle.

Simon had uncles on Scott's side of the family, but because of distance and money he saw little of them, and he barely knew his cousins. Linc was a constant in his life, someone he trusted, and someone he could talk to.

Linc made the effort to be there for the little things that might someday become real memories. He and his wife were there for Simon's first T-ball game. They flew across the country to see his eighth grade band perform in a state Battle of the Bands tournament. Linc was there when eighteen year old Simon was awarded his black belt in karate.

He was there for Simon's graduation from college, the bearer of a bottle of expensive wine and a massively loaded Visa gift card for his godson.

Simon was twenty two; while I still had problems remembering my little boy was old enough to drink, Linc did not, and he didn't hesitate getting the boy just a little bit tipsy.

"When I was four years old," Linc said as he swirled the wine in his glass, "my brother grabbed me by the hand and walked me across three streets to get to our church. He found two nuns in the chapel, and tried to convince them that our parents wanted him to sell me to them."

Simon snorted a laugh. "How old was he?"

"Also four...we're Irish twins, only ten months apart. But he was still the big brother, and I did anything he told me to do."

"So...how much did he get for you?"

"He asked for ten dollars and settled for five. One of the sisters told him to sit down while she went to get some money, and oddly enough less than five minutes later my dad was stomping in, and I was the one getting chewed out."

"Maybe they really did want to sell you," I offered.

"Funny. I was being yelled at because I'd been told I wasn't allowed outside the yard for any reason, and I should have known Joey would just try to get me into trouble."

"Linc, you were four years old," Simon said.

"So was Joey, but he was always a little immature. Even that young I was expected to the responsible one."

"Parental logic at its finest," Simon said, repeating one of my most common sayings, something I coughed up whenever I felt I needed to justify something stupid I'd done to him.

"Hey, you had logical parents," Scott insisted.

"Oh yeah, I figured out your particular brand of logic when I was seven or eight years old." He looked at Linc. "Things like 'I don't see why not' and 'maybe' meant no. 'Can we go to Burger King later?' 'Maybe.' 'Can I get a Nintendo for my next birthday?'

'I don't see why not.' It always meant no, but I don't think they realized it meant no."

Linc was sympathetic. "I got 'ask Santa.' I think my parents didn't want to come right out and say no because they hoped that I'd either forget what I asked for, or that by the time Christmas rolled around they'd be able to afford my current whim."

"Naw," Scott said, "we only wanted to mess with his little head."

"Did a good job," Linc snorted.

"Besides," I added, "we figured it out, Simon. Once we realized we kept almost-promising things we couldn't deliver, we stopped avoiding giving you answers."

"And that's when we found out that going to Burger King didn't mean you wanted to eat there," Scott said.

"I just wanted to play on the indoor playground," Simon said. Then to Linc, "Jesus, don't let your kids play in those things. They're about as gross you could imagine. Kids pee in the tubes, barf in the ball pits..."

Scott nodded. "Simon found a syringe in one once."

"You could have shared this tidbit before my kids hit five years old, you know," Linc said.

Linc's kids were all under ten; while Scott and I popped Simon out before my twenty second birthday, Linc and his wife suffered through years of wanting kids and not having them. No one was surprised when the Fertility Fairy finally graced them and they had three kids in four years; he swore he wanted ten little boys and girls running around his house, while his wife swore she'd rip his gonads off if she had to pop out more than four.

When his daughter turned three, Linc realized he had more than he could handle.

"Forget the terrible twos," he said then. "She hit three years old and...holy crap. She's like this miniature teenager already. I can't believe so many opinions can come out of that little mouth and that she's already rolling her eyes at us."

They stopped at three. Linc's wife didn't mind not having a fourth, and mused that if Scott and I kicked the bucket, they would always have Simon.

That was funny until I found myself hanging upside down in a crushed car.

I'd mostly forgotten about the Burger King excursions. Once we owned up to not being able to afford taking him for fast food on a whim, he sucked in a deep breath and said, "I just want to go there and play with my friends. And the crowns are free."

That's all he wanted. On cold days his friends gathered to play on the BK indoor playground, and he wanted to go, too. If we'd ever bothered to go beyond telling him "maybe" we might have known that.

A week after our parental epiphany

Simon repeated his request—Scott had taken him to play and Simon came home with his free cardboard crown—but this time he added, "and can I get a soda? I know you got paid yesterday."

All he wanted was sixty cents of Scott's paycheck to buy a small soft drink. I had a coupon ripped from the base newspaper; we took Simon for an afternoon of swinging around the least possible hygienic (but, he swore, the most fun) playground in a ten mile radius, where the noise he and his friends created resulted in a bottle of Tylenol shared between tired parents, and we capped it off with Junior Whoppers and fries, leading Simon to declare it the Best Afternoon Ever.

It became a winter payday ritual, and the more often we took him the more we realized his friends were riding in the same boat: they were only there to play, and the burgers were a Payday Event.

"I kind of miss that," Simon said. "We must have done that for four or five years."

The ritual lasted through two different air force bases, until Simon and his friends were too big for the playground, and too cool to be seen hanging out with their parents.

Scott offered to take Simon to the nearest Burger King, where he would buy him a full sized Whopper and, if he was really good, a chocolate shake.

Simon shook his head sadly. "They just don't have playgrounds like they used to. It wouldn't be worth it."

"We could grab your Mom's wheelchairs and take them to Costco," Linc said. "She says racing through the aisles there is at least five kinds of fun."

"Until someone gets hurt," I added. "Those little old ladies don't jump out of the way fast enough."

"And then we could have hot dogs and churros at the snack bar," Scott said, as if he was truly considering it. He looked at me and added, "Surely we can plop you down on a bench somewhere."

"Gee, thanks."

"Come on," Linc teased. "Haven't you ever let them play with your wheels?"

I started to say no, but Simon's face flushed.

"Right after you got the purple chair," he explained, "one of my friends and I borrowed the old one every now and then."

"For?" Scott prompted.

"There was that theater downtown...if you were in a wheelchair they let you and an escort in for free, because they didn't think they were fully accessible. We probably saw twenty free movies before I was miraculously cured."

Linc was snickering; Scott was mildly irritated.

"What cured you?" I asked.

"We moved."

Scott was shaking his head. "Boy, if you were a few years younger..."

Simon grinned and turned towards Linc. "Mom is going to visit her parents next week," he said, changing the subject. "Can you believe it? Mizz I'll-fly-when-I-sprout-wings is actually getting on an airplane."

I saw the look cross Linc's face: he kept his smile, but his eyes went dark and there were lines of worry creased on his forehead.

"Just securing myself in any future inheritance," I said. "I need to make sure they remember who I am."

"I'll be an hour southwest of Sacramento next week," he said. "If you need to be rescued, call me."

Simon laughed, but Scott sighed with a measure of relief. He wouldn't be able to get to me if the visit made my family implode, but Linc would be close enough to swoop in and get me home.

There was no backing out at that point.

37.

"It's a giant lipstick tube hurtling through the air at a bazillion miles an hour. The only thing between me and the great outdoors is about an inch of pounded-upon steel and a seat belt I wouldn't even count on in a car. That and the bulkhead in front of me, I think I get to sit in behind the bulkhead. Don't expect me to be happy about this."

Scott tried to force a smile. "I'd go with you if I could."

No, he wouldn't, not unless someone was dying; his patience with my family ran out just after Simon turned five, when my mother tried to bribe him with cookies and a TV for his bedroom if he would start begging for a baby brother or sister. Simon—who in his post-toddler wisdom agreed to his grandmother's terms, insisted on the TV up front and then ratted her out— would have gone if not for the realities of life

at a new job, being low man on the work-
place totem pole without a single vacation
day in the bank.

So I was going. Alone. To see my family
before either of my parents had the chance
to die and leave me with an inheritance of
guilt.

"Tucker is going to meet me at the airport," I told Scott, as if he didn't know.

"Your mom would be there if—"

"—if my chair would fit in her car and if
she wasn't four hundred years old. I know,
she keeps falling all over herself apologizing
for it."

Neither of us wanted to dwell on the fact
that Ev could have picked me up, and the
chair would have fit in the trunk seat of her
brand new, paid-for-by-Dad Sonata.

They wanted to see me, but to actually
go out of the way to pick me up? Why not
simply guilt the eldest grandson into driving two hours to cart his wayward aunt to
their home, just twenty minutes from the
airport.

"I still can't believe Ev wanted you to
take a taxi," Scott muttered with an exasperated sigh.

I couldn't believe that surprised him.

As long as I continued to not visit, Ev
was the Golden (sterling silver?) Child. She
reaped parental sympathy for her failings,
which she wore like a jeweled crown. She

wrapped herself in the injustices of how the world treated her, reveling in the attention the dramas shined on her. She was the one Mom could sit down with at the kitchen table and talk to for hours on end. She was there when Kel could only pop in once a week. She was there when I was not.

Once I was there, I was no longer the selfish, ungrateful spawn who refused to acknowledge their existence.

Once I was there, they'd all be able to see the pain, and Ev's particular brand of pathos might not be so special anymore.

"If you need to leave early, you can," Scott reminded me as I wheeled myself towards the gate. "Your ticket is opened ended and you can get on the first plane available. And Linc will be just two hours away. Call him and he'll drop everything to come get you, you know he will."

I knew all this, but I let him sputter on.

"You don't have to tell them they're driving you nuts. I'll call you every day, and you can use me as an excuse. Make something up."

"I'll tell them you're pregnant."

"Funny."

I stopped just short of the gate. "I don't really want to do this, Scott."

"I know."

"And I doubt I'd hate myself forever if I didn't go."

"I know that, too."

"Then tell me why I'm going."

He handed me my carryon bag. "Because you need to talk to them, Sam. You need to know why."

Why, what, I didn't need to ask.

I knew why.

38.

It's a good thing, Sam. You're going to see family, not to your own execution.

"It feels like I'm headed for a funeral, one I should care about but don't."

You care. You just don't know that you care. Once you get there and view the body, so to speak, you'll feel it.

"The last funeral I went to, I suffered a horrible case of the giggles. I had to hide in the back so I could escape to the foyer."

Then it'll be like that. You'll feel inappropriate the entire time you're there, but you'll laugh.

"I'm going to blindside them."

You don't really need to do that, you know.

"But I do. I need to know why."

What if you don't like the answer?

"Then I'll have done my grown up duty of presenting myself to my parents for inspection, they can see that I'm not six shades of weird, and that being in a wheelchair did not also cause hair to spring forth from my eyeballs, nor does it make small children wet themselves in fear when they see me rolling towards them. I can suck it up, leave, and never go back."

You don't plan on going back anyway, do you?

"No, because I can't imagine that any answer they give will be good enough."

39.

Ev couldn't help herself. She stared as I rolled myself across the living room, and as she followed me she pushed her foot against the tracks the wheelchair made in the carpet.

"They're not permanent," I told her. "Vacuum once and they vanish. It's like magic."

"It's new carpet," she mumbled, distracted by the task at hand.

"And we can vacuum new carpet," Mom said. "Stop it, Ev. You're embarrassing your sister."

Ev didn't care whether it embarrassed me or not. She tilted her head as she studied the wheelchair, squinting and blinking as if the matter was of great importance. "Are those wheels clean?" she asked. "I mean, don't you grind dirt into your carpets at home?"

"Wood floors. But I bribe Simon into

coming over twice a week to get on his hands and knees and scrub them with a toothbrush."

"Ev, would you feel better if you washed her wheels?" Mom asked, her lips twisted against the smirk she was fighting, both amused and annoyed with her middle child. "You can do my shoes while you're at it, because I'm sure I've stepped into some nasties this week."

We were sitting at the table, but Ev's stare was fixated on the carpet. "It's just that a week of that—"

"Won't hurt a thing," Mom sighed. "Do you think I care that much about the carpet, Ev?"

Ev and I both knew that she did, but she wasn't going to admit it, not after the years of pleading for me to just be there. She would wait to agonize over streaks of dirt and the haphazard maze of lines left in the weave of her perfect brand new blue carpet. If the visit went well, I might share with her the news that running ice cubes over the ruts would bring them right back up.

She had been warned. *My chair is probably going to hit corners as I go around them and it might leave marks. I might put ruts in your carpet. And God knows how I'm going to get into the bathroom, because I'm pretty sure the doors won't be wide enough to get my chair through.*

My mother set a Diet Pepsi on the table in front of me, and I realized we'd never addressed that issue once I called to say I was coming...how the hell *was* I going to get into the bathroom?

With that thought came the sudden urge to pee. I popped the top open on the can and took a deep breath, hoping I had time before I needed to test the width of the hallway bathroom door.

"How was the flight?" Mom asked, voice betraying her nerves. "Did they make you take off your shoes or anything before you got on the plane?"

Ev twisted in her chair to look at my feet. "You wear shoes?"

"Security searched me the same as everyone else," I answered my mother, "and Ev...really, 'you wear shoes?' Why wouldn't I wear shoes?"

"Well, it's not like you walk..."

"You have a brain?" I had to make a concentrated effort to not roll my eyes. "It's not like you think."

Mom's mouth gaped open, but anything she had to say to stop whatever was about to explode right in front of her was stopped by Ev's grin and muted laughter.

"It's just one of those stupid things that rolls through your head right before you fall asleep," Ev said. "Does Sam spend a lot of time trying on shoes? Does she need arch support? Does she even *know* if she needs arch support?"

"It's nice that you contemplate my feet."

"I think about other things. Like if you can drive. Did you have to give up bowling? Can you get into the bathtub by yourself? Does Scott get annoyed with having to push you around?"

"I can drive. I gave up bowling, though I still could, technically. I can roll into our shower. And no, but he doesn't have to push me often. He likes to pile packages on top of me when we shop."

"You're a pack mule."

"Is that a nice way of saying I'm an ass?"

"Well."

"Kel will be here later," Mom said quickly. "She wanted to be here when you got here, but something at work…" She was fumbling with the pop top on her soda can, looking everywhere but at me.

Ev had no problem looking at me. "She hasn't seen you in fifteen years, but a missing decimal point on someone's spreadsheet couldn't wait."

I refrained from pointing out that I hadn't seen Ev in fifteen years, either, but that didn't stop her from wanting me to take a taxi from the airport and it certainly didn't bother her that her nephew chewed off an entire day to be my chauffeur.

"Work first," Mom sighed. "That's always

it with Kel. Even before the Tucker was grown, if it wasn't school, it was work. I'm surprised he didn't grow up to be some kind of delinquent."

"Even after she got married?" I asked.

"Oh, they both work like there's no tomorrow," she sighed. "I don't think she saw more than two or three of Tucker's football games, and she barely made it to his graduation."

"If it's not a decimal point it's a password someone can't remember," Ev added. "It's always something."

I knew Kel's job was time consuming. After she graduated she worked in a bank until she was hired at a private firm specializing in forensic accounting. I'd never heard of it before she emailed to tell me she landed her dream job, but was impressed as hell; Mom was terrified until she realized that Kel's job had nothing to do with dead people.

"Tucker didn't seem to mind, but she has missed out on so much. I remember going to so many of your things, Sam. I loved the Christmas choir programs, all those kids singing their little hearts out."

"You didn't like the basketball games," Ev pointed out.

"I didn't understand the game! But at least I was there. I wonder how many times Tucker looked up into the stands to try to find his mother, and couldn't."

"I doubt he was looking," I said. "His mind was probably on the game."

"But to know your own mother can't make the time."

"Scott missed a few of Simon's games and Simon was fine with it. He understood that his dad had to work."

"Oh, that's different."

Of course it was different. It was Kel. By virtue of gender she was to shoulder the blame for not being there to see Tucker's ass warm the bench; if she'd lacked boob and been gifted with facial hair and a giant Adam's apple, it would have been different, because then she would have been the man providing for his family, not the mom too distracted by the almighty dollar to be at every single little league and high school game.

In twenty minutes we were right back where we'd left off.

I wanted to burn that kitchen table, and dammit, I had to pee.

40.

This is going well.

"So well I'm hiding in the bedroom, hoping they forget that I'm here."

It didn't take long for the Kel bashing to begin.

"And I fell right into it. What the hell is wrong with me?"

Aside from being human?

"Why didn't I defend her? I could think of a dozen reasons why she does the things she does, but I kept my mouth shut."

Didn't want to start a fight in the first five minutes?

"Or I'm just a chicken shit with no guts to follow through."

I'm pretty sure chicken shit is defined by not having guts.

"Go away."

And miss all this?

"You wouldn't be missing anything. But I bet if you wandered out there right now you'd find my mom and Ev sitting at the table, talking about how rude I am for going off to be by myself for a few minutes on the first day I'm here."

If I went out there, your mom would have a heart attack and Ev would pee herself.

"They wouldn't see you. Only I have that particular honor."

Honor or affliction?

"Take your pick, ghost boy."

What about Dad?

"He looks tired. Confused. I don't think he remembered I was coming, and even then it took a moment for him to register who I am...he's gotten old, a lot older than I expected."

Still hiding out in the den?

"I don't take it personally."

Perhaps you should.

"There's no point. He's always hidden himself away. He doesn't mean anything by it. He saw me, saw I'm really okay, but he doesn't know how to talk to me, or anyone else for that matter, so he goes and hides. I won't take it personally because it's not personal."

Wow, someone who goes and hides when he doesn't know how to handle the situation. Imagine that.

"I'm not hiding. I'm just getting a second wind."

You're hiding, Sam. You hid for fifteen

years by virtue of the Air Force moving Scott so often. Now you're hiding in a bedroom. But you're hiding, and you need to stop.

41.

There was white wine. Someone was drinking Amaretto, a lot of it. I sipped at a glass of Mountain Dew laced with a microscopic bit of vodka, not wanting to make an issue out of mixing alcohol with pain medications. As long as I had a glass sitting on the table at my elbow, I didn't think anyone would notice I wasn't really drinking.

No one should care, but someone would.

"Sam was surprised," Ev was telling Kel. "She didn't think we would consider the little things, but we did!"

Kel's lips pursed in amusement over her drunken sister's excitement. Hurray, they had put their heads together and figured out a way for Sam to pee, before Sam even got there. It was a Gold Star moment, and if Ev had had a chart on which to stick one, she would have waited impatiently for her sparkly little reward.

I did appreciate how their minds worked.

They borrowed a wheelchair from a neighbor and rented another. One was in the bathroom and one was in the bedroom; all I needed to do was shimmy up to the door, transfer my fat ass from one chair to the other, and I was in.

Their inventiveness deserved credit; I was prepared to abandon my chair at the bathroom door and shuffle in agony across the floor to the toilet, and I was seriously considering not showering for a week.

Pondering how Sam was actually going to take a shower was not on their List Of Things To Figure Out; I could get into the tub, turn the water on, and sit there under a spray of water, but I wasn't exactly sure how I was going to get out without hand rails and neither of them looked strong enough to help me.

"Do the chairs fit?" Kel asked me.

"Fit?" Ev screwed up her face. "Chairs 'fit'?"

"My ass has to fit in them," I said to Ev. And then to Kel, "Close enough. They work and that's all that matters."

"I never thought about fit," Ev mumbled, deflated that she might not deserve more than a silver star.

"I couldn't fit in a sixteen incher," I said, "but an eighteen is just about perfect."

"What happens in a sixteen incher?"

"The sides of her thighs get caught in

the wheels," Kel snorted, a little on the tipsy side herself. "Is it like rug burn, or does it feel like the chair bites?"

"It bites, definitely."

Ev's eyes brightened. "Oh! Like when the toilet seat cracked and it pinched my ass!"

"Pretty much like that," I agreed.

Mom sighed, and reached for the bottle of Amaretto. "It's been how long since we saw this girl, and you're talking about toilets and getting your ass pinched."

"Could be worse," Ev said. "We could be asking her how she gets from the chair onto the can…"

"It's easy enough," I started.

"Sam. I don't need to picture that. You're only here for a few days and there are more important things to talk about."

"What do you want to talk about?" Kel asked.

"I want to talk about why Sam is here," Mom said, looking at me. "I want to talk about Steven."

42.

It was a sucker punch to the head, delivered when my eyes were closed and not expecting so much as a finger flicked in my direction.

I was supposed to bring up Steven.

I was supposed to rant and rave and demand answers.

Not Mom.

"Who?" Ev asked, blinking against the vodka fog that was wrapping around her brain.

"Steven," she repeated. "Your brother."

Kel set her drink down, just as puzzled as Ev, and started to ask "Our what?" when the pieces fell into place.

I'd never heard Mom refer to Steven as our brother. It was always by name, or "the boy," and I hadn't heard her mention him at all since his death.

The light bulb went off in Ev's head. "Oh,

him! That grimy little kid who lived with us for a couple of years."

"That kid was your brother," Mom said firmly. "And you forgot about him."

My heart was pounding and I couldn't get my mouth open long enough to point out that she had made it easy for Ev and Kel to forget. Kel had never lived with him and only met him two or three times, and Ev routinely—without parental objection—ignored him. I could forgive Kel for not having Steven on her radar, but Ev...she was just Ev. Too self absorbed to hold onto anything that didn't directly impact her.

Kel started to apologize, but Mom waved her off. "You didn't really know him," she said quietly. "For you I would imagine he's like that third cousin six times removed. You know the cousin exists, but..."

She glanced at Ev, and then looked back at me. "But Sam...they were like twins, and I'm willing to bet there's not a day that goes by that she doesn't think about him."

I nodded, still a little numb.

"That's why you're here, Sam?" Ev asked. "Because of some guy who died when you were a teenager?"

"She was twenty," Mom said softly. "And she loved him, and still misses him. He mattered to her, Ev."

I wanted to snap *unlike to you?* but I still couldn't find my voice.

"But still, he's why you came, Sam? Not to see us? We're your *family*."

"So was Steven," Mom said.

"But he's *dead*. What's the point in coming here for someone who's dead when there are people who are alive who have wanted to see you for fifteen goddamned years?"

Kel was shaking her head. "Shut up, Ev."

"Like hell. She couldn't be bothered to come see us for *years!*"

"And you wanted to go see her how many times?" Kel pressed. "You never made the effort, either, Ev, you never once mentioned the possibility of going to see your younger sister, so shut up. Whatever reason got her here, it got her here and we get to see her." She turned to me, pushing her glass of wine away. "I am really sorry I let him slip my mind, Sam. I knew you two were close. It's inexcusable."

"It's all right," I wanted to tell her. "Mom is right, you didn't know him, you probably don't remember what he looked like or how his voice squeaked and popped for the first year he lived with us. You didn't have the chance to miss his laughter and wonder where he got that amazing singing voice. You didn't get to see him laugh so hard he was afraid he would wet himself."

I wanted to say that, but I didn't.

"Son of a..." Ev was still winding up, and

we let her go. "I've been your sister for your entire life and he was only the guy down the hall for what, two or three years? He matters and we don't? It's not like he's here, Sam. He's not even buried here; his body is rotting in some hole in Texas. Why the hell did you even come?"

"She came because her heart has been broken for over twenty five years," Mom said softly, "and it's my fault."

43.

She wanted to show me something; we
left Kel and Ev at the table, still arguing in
harsh whispers over what my intentions had
been when I called and said I was finally
coming for a visit, and she led me into the
den. I expected my dad to be there, a book
propped up on his beer belly while he half
watched CNN, but the bedroom door was
closed and I could hear him snoring.

I transferred from my wheelchair to his
desk chair, and she pushed me across the
room to the wall of bookcases beside Dad's
desk. The shelves were loaded with old hard
back books, most of the dust jackets missing, and the occasional empty space was
filled by a framed photograph or a random
nick-nack given to him by Simon or Tucker.

In between a thick book about Harry S
Truman and an equally massive tome on the
generation surviving the Second World War
was Tucker's kindergarten Father's Day

project, a mass of glue and macaroni with four toothpicks sticking out at odd angles. "It's you!" he had proudly squealed when Dad opened it.

Ev and I called Dad 'Macaroni Man' for weeks after, amused by his apparent embarrassment.

Mom reached for a picture frame and handed it to me. "This is our favorite picture of the two of you. You were both laughing so hard I was afraid one of you would stop breathing."

Steven and I were hanging off each other, mouths open in wild glee. I couldn't have told her what was so funny, or even when it was taken.

"It was the first time you celebrated a birthday together," she explained. "You decided since you were both turning thirteen so close to each other that you wanted to share a birthday party. Steven had a whoopee cushion, and your Dad sat on it."

I remembered. Dad sat down to a loud *fwap*, and we both broke out in hysterical laughter when instead of scowling and getting mad, he waved a hand as if clearing the air, and then blamed Mom.

She blamed the dog that we didn't have.

"We were so worried that you two wouldn't get along and that you would hate him, yet within just a few days he was your best friend. I don't think I ever heard you laugh as much as when you were with him. I know you didn't laugh much after, at least not until Scott came into your life."

She took the picture and looked at it for several long, quiet moments, and sucked in a deep breath as she placed it back on the shelf. "I wanted him to be happy and at first I thought he would be, especially when he acted like you'd been his sister all along."

"Then why—?"

"I didn't know what to do with a twelve year old boy, Sam. He was hurting and he wanted his mother, and I knew I would never be that for him. I would never measure up to someone he missed so much…I just didn't know what to do with him."

"So you pretty much left him to his own devices."

"I let him think I was leaving him alone. But I usually knew what he was up to."

"Football, baseball…did you know how well he could sing and dance and how much he wanted someone to notice?"

"Do you know how many games I went to and hid in the upper bleachers so he wouldn't see me there? Or how much I loved sitting in the living room when he was in his bedroom practicing his guitar, listening to him sing? Do you realize it broke my heart when he didn't want to move with us?"

That was a verbal sucker punch to the chest, and I resented it.

"Are you freaking kidding me? He felt like he'd been abandoned! He was barely feeling settled and all the sudden we're moving and not taking him with us—"

"He didn't want to go, Sam."

"Mom, come on!"

She sat in Dad's chair carefully, as if it might break under her weight. "When your dad found out he was being transferred, we decided Steven needed to have a choice. He never seemed happy with us—"

"He never felt wanted."

"—so we decided to give him that choice. He could come with us, or stay in Texas. He opted to stay in Texas."

"Why would he stay there? You shoved him into a family he barely knew and ripped him apart from someone who really did want him around. *I* wanted him around, Mom. I *needed* him around."

Her head tilted, and she scrunched her eyebrows together. "Sam, it's not like we left him with total strangers. We left him with his aunt and uncle."

"You left him with the vice principal," I spat.

"Robert was his mother's brother. We didn't just abandon him, we left him with people who already loved him and had wanted him all along. If we'd known how miserable he was going to be with us, your father would have given Rob custody from the day Steven's mother died. It wasn't fair for us to take him in the first place, but—"

"How long did you know about him?" I asked suddenly.

"About Steven? I knew before he was born, Sam."

"So you knew Dad cheated on you, and you never said anything about the son that came from it?"

"Not that my marriage is any of your business, but yes, I knew. We had some rough patches, and we handled it badly, but your Dad never lied about any of it to me, and he loved his son, no matter what you think."

"I never doubted that he did. But I was pretty sure you hated Steven."

She sighed hard. "I was not very good for him. He deserved so much better...I didn't know how to care for a boy who didn't want me. I cared about him, but I didn't know how to care *for* him."

"Not ignoring him would have been a start."

"I know."

"Why didn't he tell me staying behind was his choice?"

"Would you have listened? You were so angry that we were moving and leaving him there. You needed someone to blame, and you couldn't blame him. I don't imagine he ever wanted to be in a spot where you would resent him for the choice that he made."

"I missed him so much…"

"But he visited you a lot." She said it as so much a matter of fact that I had to stop and think.

"Wait. You knew about that?"

She allowed herself a soft smile. "Sam, he was just a boy. How do you think he had the money for all those trips? His uncle paid for his first visit, and when your dad realized how much it meant to both of you, he kept an account open for Steven to use."

I started to open my mouth but she added, "Steven didn't know where the money came from."

"He should have. It would have meant everything to him."

"He wouldn't have used it if he had known, and then you wouldn't have seen him so often. None of us were happy with the idea of him flying alone and staying in motels alone, but if he hadn't, you both would have been so miserable. He never would have asked to stay here with us."

"He would have presumed the answer would be no. *I* would have presumed the answer would be no. We never had a clue he would be welcome."

"I'm admitting it. We didn't handle anything with him very well. We were horrible parents for him, and for that I'll never forgive myself. I hoped that someday we'd at least come to a friendly impasse. I kept thinking that as he got older, we would have a chance to be a family, even if it was an odd kind of family."

"But then he died."

She swallowed hard, and nodded. "Your kids aren't supposed to die before you do, especially when you've failed them miserably. We never had the chance to tell him how sorry we were, and how we wished we'd done it all differently. It felt like one day he was fine, the next he was sick, and then he was gone."

"The Brownings didn't tell you?"

"Steven was an adult by then. They had to abide by his wishes. So did you. I expect he told you long before he told your dad."

"He thought he could beat it."

"Oh, I wish he had. I'd give almost anything to be able to look at him one more time, and tell him he was wanted. That his dad loved him and I would have, too, if I'd had more time and half a clue."

"You missed out on a lot," I ventured.

"Other than a few pictures Rob sent, I never got to see him as a young man. I wanted to see him happy, finding someone who loved him."

"He had a few girlfriends," I said.

"But did he have time to find the right one? Someone who would have loved him for the next eighty years?"

I didn't think Sasha counted.

"You have every right to be angry, Sam. We gave you a brother and for all intents and purposes took him away. I was always afraid to talk about him, and if I'd so much as breathed out his name…"

I didn't know what else to say.

She had loved Steven. She just didn't know it.

44.

My mother was near tears and I was choking on my own realizations—she loved Steven, she had wanted Steven—so we didn't hear the bedroom door creak open or see Dad until he was in the room and standing beside me.

"If I could have died in his place, I would have, Samantha," he said in a near whisper. "If I could go back and do things differently..." He sat down on the footstool near my mother, and for a moment he fussed with the hem of his pajama pants. "We would have stayed in Texas. If I'd thought for one minute that he only had a few more years to live...I might have let him go live with Rob and Sharon, but we would have stayed in Texas. And that's selfish because if we hadn't moved you never would have met Scott and there would be no Simon...but if I could do it again, I would stay in Texas and see the last five years of my son's life."

No Scott. No Simon. No hushed, wild giggles in the middle of the night, hoping Scott's roommate wouldn't hear. No first steps of tiny feet or hearing a little boy's first words be an entire sentence of "I want dat."

Would I trade them for Steven's last years?

My father would. The pain of losing his son would make that choice for all of us.

Steven's mother hadn't known at first that he was married. She only knew that there was something between them, that he had noticed her in the office and he enjoyed talking to her. He didn't admit to himself where they were headed, and even though he knew it was wrong, he did nothing to stop it.

"I was miserably unhappy back then, Sam. I didn't know why and I didn't know how to fix it, so I just stepped back and let my whole life derail."

Within two weeks, it was over. He'd woken up to the ugliness of what he was doing, he saw a doctor, saw a shrink, and began swimming through the depression that had clouded his life. He'd started to see light in things, and was overjoyed when Mom told him she was pregnant again.

Two days later he found out he was going to be a father twice over, and he realized he was headed back into the darkness that had left him so confused before.

It was swimming against a riptide, and if not for knowing he would never forgive himself for letting two new lives plunge into the depths with him, he would have stopped swimming.

"I had already told your Mom what I'd done. Now I had to tell her about a baby that never should have been." He looked up at Mom, then at me. "There was no clean choice of ending it in those days. It was possible, but it was nasty and hurtful and illegal, and women died... But she offered. She didn't want to complicate anyone's life. Not mine, and not hers. Being a single mother meant facing fingers pointing from all directions...her life would have been easier if she'd gotten rid of him."

"But obviously she didn't," I said.

He nodded. "She would have. But your Mom—" he looked up at her again "—she went to see her, and talked her into keeping the baby."

"Are you freaking kidding me?"

"That baby was innocent," Mom said. "And just because your dad made a mistake, that didn't mean she should have to give up being that baby's mother. She wanted him, Sam. I could see it in her eyes. She talked of how hard it would be, but her eyes..."

"What did you tell her?"

"That your dad was a little numb, but if

she would give him time, he would want that baby as much as he wanted all his babies. He would do his best to be a father to it, as much as she wanted him to. And if she really didn't want to be its mother, then if she would have it, we would take it and raise it and love it... God, I don't mean 'it.' I would have said him if we'd known it was a boy. But we would have taken Steven at birth if she had wanted us to. And I'm sure I would have been able to raise him as my own. Your dad and I talked about how you two would be like twins...and we were right, for the most part you were like twins."

"Then why didn't we know about him? Why was he a secret for twelve years?"

"Because I'm an idiot," Dad said. "I thought I was protecting everyone and keeping them from being shamed by what I did. And you don't have to say it, because I know. I was protecting myself. I didn't want you and your sisters to hate me and I was afraid that you would."

In my head I was screaming that we were all just children then; we wouldn't have hated him because we wouldn't have known life any differently. And how long did he expect to keep his son a secret? Another five years? Ten? Did he hope we wouldn't discover Steven until we were all standing around his grave, mourning the loss of our common father?

Instead, I quietly asked, "When she died, why didn't he just go live with his uncle then?"

"Because he was my son, Sam. I'd had twelve years of loving him from a distance, and I wanted my son. I hoped over time he would realize that I loved him."

"He did know that," I said softly. "He never doubted it."

"We had no way of realizing how much Ev would resent him," Mom said. "I don't think she said more than a few words to him for two years. God, we raised such a little bitch in that one."

"Mom!"

"Well come on, Sam! She never has anything nice to say about anyone. Even when she's happy she complains about everything. She talks about wanting jobs but she doesn't do much to get them, and when she actually does, the whole world is out to get her."

"Been waiting a long time to get that out?" I snickered.

Dad got up, kissed me on the head, and left the room. He looked beaten down and horribly sad, but there wasn't a thing I could say to him.

It was pounding in my head: *Steven didn't want to go. Steven wanted to stay in Texas. Steven didn't have the heart to break mine.*

"Ev is who she is, Mom," I said. "You

can only do so much to warp your children into what you want them to be. My son is obstinate and opinionated, and very nearly always right, but try to argue with him...cripes."

"Like his mother?"

She had me there. "Like his mother. But I'd hoped he'd learn to temper that with being a little more open minded."

"But he will be. You get out of your kids what you pour into them. We coddled Ev horribly, and it shows. By the time you came around, we had learned that the world is unpredictable and we needed you to be ready for it. And look at you—you can handle anything."

I wished that were true, but my massive ego let it go.

"I have to ask you something," I said with a bit of a sigh, "since we're talking about mistakes."

She waited.

"I hate your kitchen table."

"What?" she sputtered with a laugh.

"All those years of sitting around it after dinner, and mostly what we did was bash Kel. We complained about babysitting, we ripped her apart for being in school and doing something to get ahead. Even now, one of the first things we did when I got here was sit at that damned table and complained about her having to be at work."

"We do talk a lot," she mused.

"But...?"

"Talking about your family is a pretty natural thing to do, I think."

"But it was always mean. I can't remember us ever having much nice to say; it was always us whining about how Kel lived her life. I hate that we did it, and I can't fathom why you allowed it."

She shrugged lightly. "Oh, Sam, that's so obvious."

"Then enlighten me."

"Kel had a wonderful little boy, a job, she was going to school and she knew exactly what she wanted to do...I was proud of her. Nothing was going to stand in her way, even if it meant taking crap from me."

"Then why?"

"I was jealous, Sam. She had so much focus and the guts to go after the things she wanted, and I was jealous."

45.

"I can't believe I tucked Steven away into the back of my brain," Kel said, swirling the ice cubes in her glass. "I know he wasn't a part of my everyday life, but still. Once I got over the shock that Dad had another kid, I was so happy that we had a brother."

"At least you didn't refer to him as 'that dead guy.'"

We were sitting on the back porch; she glanced into the kitchen through the window. Ev was still at the table, flipping through a magazine, and I wondered for just a moment if there was a marketable skill in that.

"I think she was dropped on her head as a baby," Kel sighed. "Probably more than once."

"She needs to get her own life."

"She won't. And they won't make her leave. I know Mom resents the hell out of her being here, but the whole situation has just been too comfortable for them all. Ev doesn't have to be a grownup, and Mom has someone to talk to."

"Dad still hides in the den with his books and TV?"

"He's no fool," she laughed.

"How can Ev be happy like this?"

"She's not. Mom's not happy, either. I know she wishes they made Ev leave thirty years ago."

"Wow. Thirty. It seems so long when you think of the actual number of years."

"It's only the last twenty five that are kind of shameful." Kel looked back, turning in her chair to look at me. "It'd be different if Ev had a decent reason for needing to stay. Some people can't live alone because they have medical problems, some need to be their parents' caretaker, some people just can't handle the loneliness or they don't make enough money. Face it, it's expensive as hell to live here now. Hell, if Ev's reason for staying was just that she really likes our parent's company, that would be fine. I can think of a lot of reasons why it would be all right. It's just that Ev's only reason for never moving out is because she's just a giant bag of Me, Me, Me."

I glanced down at my chair. "I could live alone."

She waved it off. "That's different. You're Sam. Sam can do anything. Mom says so at least once a month."

"You've got to be freaking kidding me. I'm like the black sheep of the family."

"No, you're the wunderkind who's been out there experiencing the world. You know all, do all, and even though you've been to hell and back, you don't let the shit get you down. With the obvious exception, any time someone brings your name up, it's like you were walking on water."

"I'd like to be walking anywhere, frankly."

She considered this. "So why don't you? You can still feel your legs, right?"

I patted my thighs. "I can feel, but mostly what I feel is pain. There's a lot of scar tissue and rough bone rubbing on other rough bone, that standing hurts so much I want to throw up. Sitting isn't much better. I spend a lot of time floating in the pool where I feel almost normal."

"They can't fix it?"

"I've had six surgeries to smooth the bone surfaces and to have scar tissue cut out, but more forms...at this point I think the only thing they can do to stop the pain is sever the nerves, and then I really would be paralyzed."

She paused to consider it, looking down at my legs. "Would that be so bad? You already don't walk; why not get rid of the pain?"

"For the same reason Mom and Dad

haven't gotten rid of theirs. Sometimes you just have to live with it. Better the devil you know that the devil you don't, or something like that."

"At least you feel something," she mused.

"Something is better than nothing."

"Is Steven the reason you came back, Sam? Is he your pain?"

"He wasn't exactly my reason for coming back," I said. "He was just my excuse for staying away."

46.

Fourteen years old; six months before we moved from Texas and left Steven behind. It was January, it was cold, and Steven refused to wear anything more than a well-worn sweatshirt with his old elementary school mascot emblazoned across the front.

Our Health Ed teacher—the baseball coach who gushed about sports stats instead of preventative health measures ninety percent of the time—found this choice in winter wear unacceptable and dragged Steven to the office, where he waited for my mother to show up in answer to the assistant principal's call. When he didn't show for our science class and wasn't in the cafeteria afterwards, I bought a candy bar and a Coke from the vending machine and went looking for him.

He was sitting on a hard wooden chair just outside the office, slouched down, his arms crossed and eyes practically rolled back into his brain. I gave him the candy bar and Coke, and asked why he was still there. It wasn't like he'd done something wrong.

"Evidently me not wearing some over-sized down jacket suggests I'm not properly cared for." He popped open the Coke and took a sip. "Thanks. Your mom is in there now."

I could hear her irritation through the door. *Steven is old enough to know if he's cold. And why should it matter to you?*

A muffled voice replied, sounding tired, probably defending a teacher he really didn't want to defend.

My son is not an idiot. And I don't appreciate him being kept out of class because he wasn't wearing a jacket inside the school building.

"Yay," Steven said weakly, "I'm not an idiot."

"Dude, you're eating a Three Musketeers candy bar for lunch and you do it every day. That doesn't suggest an extremely high level of brain activity."

"And who bought it for me?"

"I'm pandering to your disgusting habits, that's all."

The door banged open and Mom stepped out; she glanced at me and then asked Steven, "Are you freezing?"

"There's ice hanging off my nipples," he replied dryly.

She turned to the assistant principal. "If you want to check his nipples, go right ahead. If he's got just one icicle hanging off even one of them, I'll march right down to the mall and buy him a jacket he'll despise wearing."

He shook his head wearily, though there was a little bit of amusement in his eyes.

To Steven she said, "If that teacher gives you any more crap about not being appropriately dressed for the weather, tell him he can come over for dinner and kiss my lily white ass."

We watched her storm off. I was awe-struck, and he was laughing.

It took me over thirty years to hear her. She called him her son.

47.

Thirteen.

Steven's heart had been battered and bruised by the head eighth grade cheerleader. He moped around the house, he plastered himself to his bed and listened to crappy songs on the radio, and he refused to talk about it.

"No one gives a shit," he glowered, "and nothing will make me feel better, so leave me alone."

I left him alone.

I didn't see the point to his misery; she was a redheaded bitch-in-training, and was in love with someone new (always from the current sports team) every other week. By Christmas break she'd had six soul mates, the boys who were going to grow up and be The One, boys who would become men who would treat her like the Queen she was destined to be.

Steven was just another disposable

hopeful. And he wasn't in love with her and barely in like; he wanted a toy, he wanted someone else's fun parts to play with, and when he didn't get it and she moved on to boyfriend #25, his ego was wounded.

Friday after a basketball game, when we normally would have gone to a friend's house to celebrate a victory or create a laundry list of Reasons Why The Refs Hate Us, he wanted to go home instead. The game wasn't mine; I was just the spectator, so I went home with him.

We walked into the house, and the air was thick with the aroma of freshly baked cookies.

Chocolate chip oatmeal with raisins. Steven's favorite. No one else liked them.

Someone gave a shit, after all, and it wasn't me.

48.

Twelve.

Steven stepped into the house, a gym bag slung over one shoulder and a suitcase dangling from the fingers on his other hand. He was pale, wide-eyed, and glanced around nervously, trying to soak in everything at once while trying to not look at any one thing.

His mother had been buried just a few days before, and now he was standing in a strange house, surrounded by curious people who wanted to get a good look at him. He stood there like a museum display, allowing everyone to stare, and he was the prisoner being guided into the place he would spend the next three years-to-life.

We gawked. Dad stood behind him silently, not pushing him any further into the house. I had run from the kitchen to see my new brother, but couldn't think of anything to say to him, not even hello. Ev wandered past, stared for a moment before rolling her eyes, and walked away.

Mom brushed past me and smiled at him, reaching for his suitcase. "Come on," she said gently, "we don't bite, no matter how rude we are."

Steven looked at her, drinking in the details of her face, taking in every fine line and graying hair. Not his mother, you could see it spinning through his head. She was not his mother. He would never see his mother again. She could be as nice as she wanted, but she was not the woman he wanted being nice to him.

She took a step back, handing the suitcase to me. The smile faded, leaving behind a grim shadow; she understood the pain that was dripping from him and she couldn't take it away as easily as she had taken the suitcase.

"Sam, show Steven his room," she said quietly, still hiding behind what little smile she could manage.

I dragged the bag alongside me, leading the way down the hall to Kel's old room. The walls has been stripped bare of anything that suggested a teenager had once lived there; there was nothing but the bed, a dresser, a night stand, and a lamp.

It was little more than a prisoner would have owned.

Steven sucked in a deep breath, dropped

the gym bag, and sat on the edge of the bed.

"You have more crap than that, don't you?"

"At home," he said softly.

"I'll help you bring it over if you want."

He shrugged. "Yeah. Maybe."

"Or if you want new crap, now's the time. I think you could get just about anything you wanted out of my parents. Your parents. Well, your Dad."

"It's okay."

"Seriously. Want a TV for your room? I bet you could get it."

Mom walked in, bearing gifts of a laundry basket and new pillows. "I think," she said, setting them on the bed, "that a small TV could be arranged."

"I'm more into music," Steven mumbled.

"All right. We'll get you a stereo, too. Anything you need, Steven."

"See?" I said when she walked out. "Guilt is a wonderful thing."

He pursed his lips thoughtfully. "I actually have a stereo. A new one would be nice, but if she goes over to my house to help get my stuff, she'll see it."

"Hell, give it to me. *I* don't have one."

"So the new kid gets the new stuff and you get crapped on with hand me downs?"

"Story of my life," I sighed dramatically. "The only thing I don't get used is clothes, but that's only because I won't wear that girly crap."

"So maybe you'll get stuck with my stuff now."

"I probably will, unless you wear girly crap."

When he brought his things over from his mother's house, he brought the stereo and the TV from their living room. He plastered his walls with old posters, and covered the floor with his dirty clothes, ignoring the laundry basket. He refused offers to wash his clothes, saying he'd been taught to do it himself, that it was one of his chores.

He never asked her for anything, other than the occasional ride to the cemetery. Later, he and I rode our bikes out there together, and he stopped asking her for even that much.

She only insisted once that I could remember; just before Christmas she pulled him away from homework and made him get in the car. I tagged along for the hell of it, and because I was willing to take any excuse to get out of studying for a history test.

After she parked the car, before he and I could wander off to his mother's headstone, she opened the trunk and asked him to help her.

He peered into the open trunk, asking what that was.

"It's a grave blanket," she said simply.

He pulled it from the trunk; it was a

mass of woven pine branches, tied together with thin wire and bright red and green ribbons, the corners rimmed with heavily cinnamon-scented pine cones.

She trailed behind us as we walked to the grave, carrying two large and bright poinsettias, and after she helped place the blanket on the ground, tucking it just so near the headstone, she quietly went back to the car. Steven kneeled in front of his mother's grave, taking it in.

"This is so nice," he said after a while. "I like that she's not going to be cold for the winter. Those are her favorite Christmas flowers, too. She used to buy dozens of them to make a little tree by stacking them up on blocks and stuff. And she loved cinnamon candles, we almost always had two or three lit…"

That was the first time it occurred to me that Christmas was going to be hard for him. And I didn't stop to think that my parents were bracing themselves for it, trying to figure out a way to make it easier.

When we got back to the car, my mother's eyes were rimmed with red, her eyelashes wet. Steven slid into the front seat, not looking at her, and he said quietly, "Thanks, Mrs. C."

I didn't understand why she was crying for someone she couldn't have possibly missed, someone she probably would have really disliked.

I never thought she was crying for Steven. I never would have guessed.

49.

It's easy to assume things, especially when you're so young. How can you expect yourself to have understood everything that was boiling just under the surface? You were twelve years old.

"I really thought she hated you. I keep trying to reach for these memories of her being nice, but I can only call up a few."

Maybe what you should be looking for are memories of me not treating her like she was fourth or fifth best. Try to find some point when I wasn't ignoring her.

"I don't get it. Why would you be the one doing most of the ignoring?"

She wasn't my mother, Sam. My mother was dead and she wasn't coming back, and I wasn't about to let someone take her place.

"She would never—"

I was twelve, too, Sam.

"She went to your games, she went to your recitals, she stood up to the school administration for you. She did all that, not Dad."

Yep. Kind of makes you wonder why, eh?

"Women take care of the kids, men bring home the paycheck. He was raised that way and lived that way. I doubt it occurred to him it should be any different."

But then there was your mother, investing herself into someone else's son's life, even when she knew she wasn't wanted.

"Did you know she was there all those times?"

Would I have ever admitted it if I did?

"She wanted you to move with us."

And yet she let me go when I didn't want to go.

"I thought I was the only one left with a broken heart over that."

If you love someone, set them free…that kind of crap. She tried for almost three years, more than most people would have, I think.

"I wonder if the adult Steven would have recognized her efforts."

Look how long it took the adult Sam.

50.

"All right, answer me this because for some stupid reason it was bugging me all last night." Kel was standing by the stove, dropping spaghetti into a pot of boiling water. "No one in this family goes by their full names. Not me, not Ev, not Sam. So why was he 'Steven'?"

I didn't know. He came into my life as Steven, and left it as Steven.

"When he was very little," Mom answered, "your Dad called him Steve once. He screwed up his little face and said 'if my Mommy wanted anyone to call me Steve, she would have named me Steve.'"

"So he was a little prick even back then?" Ev offered.

Mom glared at her for a moment, and then turned in her seat so that Ev was almost to her back. "He had definite opinions from the time he could talk."

"Did you ever meet him or see him before he moved in?" I asked.

She nodded. "A few times, but your dad didn't have as much time with him as he would have liked, and I didn't want to intrude on what little time they did have together."

I couldn't imagine my father taking a little boy fishing, or out for pizza or ice cream. He'd never done that with any of us, and I felt a tiny stab of pain that someone else got that kind of attention from him.

As soon as the feeling hit I mentally slapped myself back into reality. If he took Steven fishing, it was a gender issue, not that he loved his girls less. He surely did guy things with his son, and simply had no clue what to do with his daughters.

Kel nodded thoughtfully. She finished stirring the pasta and sat down at the table with the rest of us. "I can't imagine how hard it was for the two of you to keep him a secret for all those years."

"Oh, you don't know that half of it," Mom said. "There were a few times we were just bursting with pride over something he had done, and we couldn't just sit here and talk about it."

"Like we would have cared when he stopped peeing himself," Ev muttered.

"One time, I think he was only in third grade, his teachers wanted to put him ahead a year...he had taken some test that they gave to all the fifth and sixth graders just for the hell of it, and he got the second highest score in the school. His mother was so proud...but in the end, he refused to skip a grade."

"You gave him the choice?"

She nodded. "Your dad and his mom decided that since it wasn't them who would suddenly be stuck in a room full of older kids, he needed to have a voice in it. But he didn't want to skip."

"Why?" Kel asked.

"Because," Mom said with a hint of laughter, "he said he'd done some thinking, and if he skipped a grade in elementary school, and quite possibly again in junior high because he was *that smart*, by the time he got to high school he'd be so much younger than everyone else that no girls would want to date him."

Ev slammed the magazine shut. "He was a little pothead, you know. You guys are getting all warm and fuzzy over someone who spent a lot of time stoned out of his mind."

Kel and Mom both stared at her.

"And you would know this, how?" I asked.

"He always smelled like it."

"And you know what pot smells like, how?" I pushed.

"Never mind!" Ev's cheeks flushed, and

she was twisting the magazine in her hands. "I smelled it on him once, and if you smell pot on someone once, you know they're doing it a lot."

"What does it smell like?" Mom pressed. "Because, you know, I've smelled an awful lot of strange things over the years, but I would never know to chalk it up to pot."

"It's like...it's like burning rope," she sputtered.

"Ev, you moron." I grabbed the magazine from her and tossed it out of her reach, just annoyed enough to want to really piss her off. "Good pot—and he would have had the good stuff—smells kind of skunky. Did Steven ever smell like a skunk?"

Kel was laughing. "All right, how does Sam know what it smells like?"

"Sam," I replied, "makes no bones about her lack of innocence. It helps with pain and I don't want to spend be eating pills all the time. I don't think it's a big deal, but if Ev here thinks Steven had a habit of it, I'd like to know how she came to that conclusion, other than one time he smelled really bad."

"Why are you all sitting here talking about some kid we barely knew and didn't even like? He's *dead!*"

Kel took a deep breath. "I think the better question is why it bothers you so much that we're talking about your brother."

"He wasn't my brother. He wasn't yours

either. He was just someone's mistake."

"I didn't know him," Kel said softly, "but he most certainly was my brother. And I regret not getting to spend time with him."

"He was my best friend," I added.

"He never should have been born."

Mom turned to her, eyes suddenly rimmed with tears. "Stop it. Just stop it. You were miserable to him when he was with us, and you forgot about him when he was gone. I'm sorry if Steven's life was so inconvenient for you, but he was *not* a mistake. He was someone's son, and we loved him."

Ev stood up. "You loved Dad's bastard son. That's just terrific."

"Why wouldn't I, Evelyn? If I can love my bitch of a daughter, why couldn't I love his bastard son?"

Ev headed for the door, but stopped just shy of it. She spun around and took one step back towards the table. "You've never loved anyone but yourself. You sit around complaining about everyone else and you do it for sport." She looked at me and said, "Sam, do you know how much she bitches about you? It's always 'Sam doesn't care about anyone else, if she did she would come visit. Sam is too caught up in her own life to remember there are people here who want to see her. Sam could find the money to come if she *really* wanted.' That's your mother, Sam. She talks about you like that."

"So?"

"*So?*"

"People talk about people, Ev," I said, more than a little surprised that was coming out of my mouth. "And for you to stand there and attack her for something you've become quite the queen of..."

"What about all the whining she did about Kel? Do you even remember sitting at this table griping about having to babysit and how much Kel was never home?"

Kel let out a tight laugh. "You think I didn't know about that? Of course Mom complained. I certainly would have. The only way I got through school was because she put herself out there and did all of that for me. *For* me, Ev. Not to me. When you're tired and dealing with someone else's kid, you complain about it, or you go completely apeshit!"

Mom shrugged sheepishly. "Well...I told Sam last night, I regret doing that, all the complaining, but honestly, I was just jealous. But it really was inexcusable."

"There is nothing," Kel said sharply, mostly to Ev, "shameful about being human. But there is something wrong with being mean just to be mean. Mom never meant to be mean, but you, Ev... you need to just grow up already."

She spun and stomped out of the room; a few seconds later we heard her bedroom door slam and her stereo go on nearly full blast.

Mom sucked in a deep breath and then let it out slowly, "Well that's going to come back and bite me in the ass."

Kel shook her head. "Ev is not going to derail the gravy train, Mom. She's immature and completely wrapped around herself, but she's not stupid."

"I just don't understand where all that bitterness comes from. Why did she hate Steven so much?"

"Because," Kel sighed, "she sees life through Ev-colored glasses. She was always the kid who didn't get it, the socially backwards little girl who never really clicked with anyone because she had no clue how to play well with others. She doesn't understand personal boundaries, and honestly doesn't think things are her fault when they are. You can't get mad at her, because she really does not understand."

I didn't have to stop to think about what Kel was saying. She was right; nothing was ever Ev's fault, but I never considered that Ev had no concept that she was ever wrong. Other than an odd one here or there, she had no friends growing up. Ev's life was lived between jobs, at home in front of the TV or at the kitchen table, a magazine in hand.

"Do you think there's something wrong with her?"

Kel shrugged. "Maybe. She reminds me of some of the kids Tucker works with. Very intelligent, but socially unaware."

"Tucker works with autistic kids, doesn't he?"

She nodded. "Autistic, and Asperger's Syndrome kids. It's like a milder form of autism."

Mom considered this for a moment. She looked towards the kitchen door, and then back down at the table. "Is it wrong," she said after a moment, "that I kind of hope there is something wrong with Ev?"

"No, because it would explain a lot," Kel said.

"And it wouldn't be my fault." Mom looked up, eyes again filled with tears. "I have made so many mistakes, and it's selfish, but I don't want Ev to be my fault."

51.

You talked almost all night long. Surely you learned a thing or two or ten.

"I learned that I was a jerkwad of a kid. That's something."

Jerkwad.

"Jerk, bitch, moron. Take your pick."

When you were little.

"Fourth-grade-little, even. Like the whole off-white sweater incident. All I remembered was how disappointed she was that I stuck out like the proverbial sore thumb and how crappy she made me feel about it. I didn't remember that she had been on my case all day to take a shower and wash my hair. I forgot that no one would stand exactly close to me up there on the risers because I probably smelled from a week and a half of no baths. The sweater wasn't as dirty as the stubborn little girl wearing it."

She still could have been more kind about pointing out the obvious to her nine year old.

"She could have."

But?

"But she wasn't. It was the end of a long hard day of dealing with Stubborn Sam, and she'd had it. People around her were whispering about the greasy-haired kid in the middle, the one no one would get near. She'd tried, I resisted on Sam-level-scales, and her feelings were hurt."

Moms get hurt feelings. Who'da thunk that?

"They're supposed to be all knowing and have the patience of six or seven saints, aren't they?"

I wonder what Simon thinks about that.

"Simon was never the obnoxious little freak that I apparently was."

Ah, I see. You've cornered the market on that.

"I was stubborn, Steven."

And Simon was never an angel. Don't make the mistake of taking everything you've had built up inside of you for the past thirty-odd years and making it your fault.

"It's not my fault. But I do have to reconcile what I remember with reality. Somewhere on my personal motherboard is one hell of a faulty memory chip."

Kids see things through eyes that don't have the benefit of complete pre-frontal lobe development.

"It's like someone edited all those key points I've wrapped my anger around."

All of them?

"Enough of them. Like my eleventh birthday."

The pizza-less, hamburger-laden, cake-witholding, shattering disappointment?

"I don't remember changing my mind a dozen times, leading right up to dinner time. I don't remember deciding on pizza, and then after she'd called the order in saying I wanted a burger after all. I don't remember pitching a fit about it, though both Ev and my Dad remember it well."

I don't think I'd forget a Sam Special, either.

"Mom thinks it was just a bad day all around. They decided to get me a fish tank, and made me stay in my room while they set it up to surprise me. Only they didn't realize I was going to be stuck in my room on my birthday for over five hours while they ran back and forth between the house and the pet store. Everyone was in a bad mood by then."

But to not let you have your own birthday cake...?

"I suppose when a kid throws her food clear across the room, splattering it on a wall, she doesn't get cake."

Temper, temper.

"I can only vaguely remember doing that now."

Did you at least like the fish?

"They were dead within a week. Evidently you don't feed them three times a day they way you do people. And you don't give them fistfuls at a time."

Imagine that.

"It's no wonder the cat was always so fat. I think I also fed her a lot when no one was looking."

Surreptitiously engorging the kitty?

"Kinda makes me wonder about me, too. I killed the fish with food, I fattened up the cat...all while no one was looking."

It's not like you gorge yourself when no one is looking, Sam.

"No, I don't shove food into my face all day, but damned if I don't haul my fat ass out to fast food lunches a few times a week. Dinner, too."

Is that going to be your new piece of gristle?

"Maybe. We'll call it Let's Examine Why Sam Goes Out To Eat So Much."

Maybe Sam just wants to get out of the house, and enjoys her independence.

"Maybe Sam just wants to *prove* her independence, and can't think of anything to do other than bounce around between all the different eateries in town."

Nothing wrong with being independent.

"Unless it makes you fat."

So you're fat. Sam, stop looking for scabs

to pick at. At some point you have to stop obsessing over life, and start enjoying it.

"Says the dead guy."

Says the dead guy who only wanted to live, and be happy.

52.

My life at five years old consisted of watching Captain Kangaroo in the morning, playing with toy after toy before lunch, running around outside in the afternoon with other kids my age from the neighborhood (under the watchful eye of somebody's older brother or sister; we weren't cut loose to terrorize the world on our own until we were at least six and a half), dinner at the table with my family every evening, and a rousing game of but-I'm-not-tired that began just before 8 p.m. and continued until someone threatened to staple my sorry ass into the bed, right around 8:45.

My entire world was on Gibson Drive, and other than occasional trips to the grocery store where I was reminded at least fifteen times to stop touching things, stop running, stop talking so loud, stop picking my nose, and to not ask for anything else lest the slumbering beast within the Mommy emerge and rip my little head off, I stayed on Gibson Drive. My sisters went off to school, but that was a remote concept tucked away in the back of my brain. That was what the big kids did, that was not what five year old Sam did.

Until that one day.

Kel did her best over the summer to play up the idea that kindergarten was at least five kinds of fun: we'd get to color and to paint, we'd get to play on the playground—with real swings and slides and teeter totters—and we'd learn tons of new things, mostly by playing.

Ev grunted in response to Kel's painting of kindergarten in such bright colors, "It's boring."

Kel read books to me, pointing out that kindergarten was the first step in learning to read all by myself; Ev made sure I understood there were other kids there, mean kids that would make fun of me on the playground. "You're kind of ugly," she said pointedly.

My mother avoided talking about it as much as possible; she relied on Kel to make me want to go, hoping I would happily latch onto the idea that I was about to enter the world of Real People, where I would begin the journey of self sufficiency and where someone else could bear the burden of telling me to stop picking my nose.

The bigger picture failed to permeate any of my tender, young gray matter; I knew what I was supposed to do all day: TV, play, eat, play, annoy, sleep. I didn't need to learn to read, because Kel did that for me. I didn't need to go anywhere to color and paint, because I did that at home. And nowhere in her vivid descriptions of Life in Kinder did Kel mention anything about watching TV after breakfast. If I couldn't spend an hour with the Captain, what was the point?

Then came the day of Shopping For School Clothes. Until that day all my clothes magically appeared in my dresser and in my closet; Kel and Ev were excited, and if Ev was actually excited about this, it was at least worthy of consideration as a curiosity.

We shopped in birth order: Kel poked through racks of discount clothing, holding shirts and skirts up to herself as she looked in the mirror, sometimes she smiled, other times she sighed and put it back. When she had chosen a basket full of things I found fairly ugly, it was Ev's turn.

Ev, too, picked through racks of clothing, but Mom was right there beside her, shaking her head no or nodding yes. Every few minutes she would pluck something from the rack and hold it up, her eyebrows raised expectantly, but never upset when Mom said she didn't like something.

I sat on the floor next to Kel, who began

to tell me about how much fun it was to pick out your outfit for the first day of school. "You can wear the prettiest dress and even tights if you want! And in the morning I'll help you with your hair...I have some beautiful ribbons that would look really nice on you."

"I'm not wearing a dress," I said simply.

Mom froze for a second, and sighed.

If I'd been a little older, I could have seen it coming.

When Ev was done loading her basket—an odd mix of everything plaid that could possibly exist—it was my turn. We walked over to the little kid's section of Sears, and my world was tipped upside down and shaken like a snow globe.

My mother began pulling dresses off the racks, holding them up to me to eyeball for size. I stood frozen in horror, until the fourth dress was pressed against me just under my chin, and I managed to squeak out, "I don't *want* a dress!"

"You're a little girl, Sam. When you start school you have to look like a little girl."

"I don't want to."

"It's about time you started looking like a little lady."

"No!"

Kel tried to help, assuring me that "all the girls will be wearing new dresses on the first day."

"Not me!"

"Dressing up is fun," my mother declared. "You're going to love it."

"Like the little freak loves anything she's supposed to," Ev muttered.

"Why can't I wear something I already have?" I pleaded, voice escalating in tandem with the fear that was quickly enveloping me. "I'll look STUPID in that!"

"You'll look pretty."

I dropped to the floor on my knees and began wailing, tears rolling down my cheeks and snot running from my nose in thick globs of gross. "I don't want to be pretty!"

Mom grabbed two dresses from the rack and shoved them into the basket. "You'll do whatever I damn well want you to do."

She turned and started to stomp off, leaving Kel to pick me up.

"Way to ruin everything," Ev seethed.

My meltdown was the first thing Dad was hit with as we sat down to dinner. Ev whined that I had destroyed the most fun day they were going to have all summer. Mom complained that I had no sense of boundaries or respect, and dammit I was going to dress like a little girl whether I wanted to or not.

Dad listened without saying anything as he ate, and when the Sam Is A Horrible Child whine-fest ended, he put down his fork and said simply, "It's Sam's first day of school, not yours. She's going there to learn, not put on a fashion show, and she won't learn if she's in a panic about her clothes. If she's more comfortable in slacks, then get her some nice slacks." He looked at me pointedly. "No jeans, not the first day. But you don't have to wear a dress unless you want to. All right?"

Mom looked like she wanted to cry; Kel hid a smile behind her hand and Ev just rolled her eyes.

"You got to play dress up with two girls already," Dad said to Mom in a harsh whisper. "Don't make Sam feel like she's odd because she can't stand that."

"I don't want Sam to be...that way."

"What way?" Ev asked.

Dad glared at her for a moment and then turned back to Mom. "Just take the dresses back, and get her a nice pair of slacks. And sneakers. Sam needs new sneakers."

If I had dared, I would have stuck my tongue out at my mother in a moment of smugness. I win, you lose, Daddy hath spoken, nyah-nyah-nyah-nyah-nyah.

The morning of my first day of kindergarten, I awoke to find black stretch pants and a new baby blue t-shirt hanging from my doorknob, and bright red Keds on the floor near my closet.

Kel bounded into my room with a brush in hand and asked, "Are you excited? You get to start school today!"

She was far too happy about something that had all the promise of a trip to the dentist.

I let her comb my hair, carefully pulling out the tiny tangles, but I refused wear the red clip-on ribbon she had to match my red sneakers.

Mom lined us all up in front of the fireplace to take a First Day Of School picture, Kel in the middle with Ev and me on either side. Then she handed Kel and Ev a brown paper bag, and when I asked why I didn't get one, she smiled and said, "You get to come home and have lunch with me! You can tell me all about your first day and how you liked it... Oh! Let's go out to lunch today, Sam-I-Am! We have to celebrate your first day!"

"Hey, now, I didn't get to go out for lunch on my first day," Kel joked.

"That's because I knew I'd get this day two more times. Sam's my baby, and this is the last first day of school we'll have."

It worked for me.

The school was a mass of screaming children and cars fighting for position near the front door. I watched as kids tumbled out the passenger-side doors of dozens of station wagons and ran towards the door, and suddenly felt my stomach twist in a knot.

"But I don't know where to go," I murmured.

Mom maneuvered the car into a tight spot off the side of the road. "It's all right, Sam. I'm going to walk you inside today and introduce you to your teacher. You don't have to go in alone."

I felt like Dead Five Year Old Walking; as I took step after step towards that old beige building, the dread began to build until I felt like I was going to implode. I wanted to tell her I didn't want to go after all, but I couldn't make myself say anything.

She guided me towards the classroom, where only two other kids were waiting. Both of them looked like they, too, wanted to throw up. We were all looking around, probably trying to figure out if it would hurt to jump out the window at the back of the classroom.

"Sam," my mother said softly, "this is Mrs. Tanner. She's your teacher. Mrs. Tanner, this is Samantha—we call her Sam for short."

Mrs. Tanner held out her hand and shook mine gently. "I'm very happy to have you as a student, Sam."

I didn't know what to say. I wanted to say that I didn't want to be her student; I wanted to go home and watch Captain Kangaroo.

Mom knelt down beside me, picking an imaginary piece of lint off my shoulder. "You're going to have a wonderful day, Sam," she promised. "I'll be back to pick you up at noon, okay?"

I know my eyes went wide. "You're not staying?"

"No sweetie. You're a big girl now and can stay here without me."

But she's a stranger! I wanted to cry. *I'm not allowed to talk to strangers!*

Mrs. Tanner put her hand on my shoulder and asked, "How old are you, Sam?"

I held up five fingers.

"Then you're definitely a big girl! I promise, you'll be fine, and I won't let anything bad happen."

"But I don't know you," I whispered.

Mom touched a finger to my chin. "It's all right. She's not a stranger. Daddy and I met her a long time ago. She was Kel's first teacher, too!"

I looked up at Mrs. Tanner, still not sure she wasn't about to sprout fangs and horns, and devour me in one good gulp.

"You know what, Sam?" Mom said softly. "Daddy was right. You need to be comfortable in school, so after we go out to lunch today, we'll go back to Sears and you can buy whatever clothes you want. But they have to be school clothes...so you have to go to school to wear them."

"I like my new shoes," I offered.

"That makes me happy. Do you think you can stay here and meet the other kids, and play on the playground today? I promise, Kel loved having Mrs. Tanner as a teacher."

"Okay."

"And if it really gets to be too hard, Kel is on the other side of the school, and Mrs. Tanner can get her."

I was formulating ways to convince Mrs. Tanner to get Kel as soon as my mom left, but the door opened and in walked Danny from down the street, older brother to little Mark, whom I would later accuse of teaching me The Dirtiest Word Ever.

Danny lit up and squealed, "Sammy!"

My mother stood up, looked at Mrs. Tanner, and sighed, "I am so sorry."

"She'll be fine."

"No," Mom said, "I'm sorry you have them together. If you had any hopes of a quiet school year, they just ended."

Mom wiggled her fingers at me as she left, and I took a desk right next to Danny, only briefly wondering about the Oh Crap look on Mrs. Tanner's face.

53.

When I was eight, maybe nine years old, I called a kid down the street a fucker, because that's what the cool kids did; they used the worst words they could think of and called each other names. It wasn't personal; it was simply a part of our growing vernacular. It could have been much worse: earlier in the week someone had called me a mother fucking asshole. I could have dumped that gem onto him, and watched his pre-pubescent little head explode.

For most of the kids littering the neighborhood, it didn't matter. Someone called you a name, used foul language for the shock value, and that was it. We tucked it away as a word we could use at a later date, bathing ourselves in crude colloquialisms. No big deal.

Except to this kid. I think his name was David. I don't really remember; he didn't live in the neighborhood long enough to stick to my gray matter, and I've known so many Davids through the years that they tend to blur together, unless I thought they were really cute or super sweet and funny.

But I'll call him David. Just because.

Don't ask me what David did to deserve my verbal punch in the face. Who knows? It could have been something as simple as farting while bending over to ties his shoes. Anything we thought was stupid was a good enough reason to use one of our nifty, newly learned curse words. I'm pretty sure I was called a mother fucking asshole because I lobbed a baseball towards second base when I should have thrown it towards the short-stop.

You just didn't need a really good reason to drop the f-bomb. Any reason would do. Ladybug lands on your hand. Well, fuck! The first grader across the street falls off his bike and scrapes his knee? Fuck, that must hurt! Cute guy tells you a stupid but funny joke? You fucker!

So it could have been anything that inspired me to tell David he was a fucker. It wasn't *personal*.

David, however, must not have been informed of the rules of Swear At Any Given Opportunity. The little fucker went and told his mom.

His mom wasted no time in calling my mom.

My mom stomped out of the house, marched down the street to find me, and stood there with her hands on her hips as if she were SuperMom, about to leap small children in a single bound.

"Did you call David *that word?*"

I did, I admitted. There was no point in lying about it when there were witnesses, especially laughing and snickering witnesses.

She pointed towards home. "Go. To. Your. Room."

Here's the thing. While she stood there being all Pissed Off Mom, she was trying not to smile. She knew the game, she probably played a much tamer version as a child. There was a protocol to parenting, however, and one of its rules was if your kid calls another kid a really bad name and he's such a little weenie he has to go crying to his mommy, well, there must be a punishment.

After I'd been in my room for twenty minutes, long enough for dread to form in the worst possible ways inside my head—I was going to be grounded for a year, I would have my bike taken away, all my jeans would be shredded and I would be forced into wearing PINK dresses for the rest of my life—she stormed in.

"You should *never* call anyone that name," she informed me. "That word is the dirtiest word there is."

Oh. Yeah, well, that's what makes it so much fun to say.

(No, I was not THAT stupid.)

"Who taught you that word?"

Now, even at eight, I knew better than to tell the truth about this. There was no way I could look up and say "You" without really pissing her off. There was no way her own brain could wrap itself around the fact that she had been swearing around me from birth. I was probably 3 days old the first time I heard that particular verbal gem.

By the time I was eight I'd probably heard it all, just not in the combinations I was learning from my friends. And I certainly didn't know what the word actually meant.

(Obviously, neither did the kid who intimated that I was having inappropriate relations with my mother.)

I wasn't admitting the truth, so I blurted out the first name that popped into my head. Mark. I heard it from Mark.

Now, logically, she should have known better. Mark was four years old and only allowed outside with either his mother or his older brother, Danny. Granted, Danny was prone to the odd bad word here or there, but Mark was not afforded that honor yet. The first time he said "Damn" it was An Event, and Danny told him to knock it off. He wasn't old enough to swear.

I blamed him anyway. I told my mother

that I learned the word Fuck from four year old Mark.

My mom told Mark's Mom.

Mark got one hell of a spanking.

Three days later, when I was allowed out of the house again, I apologized to him. It wasn't his fault that I got caught calling David a fucker. And I knew I shouldn't have said I heard it from him. I felt really bad that he'd been spanked for it.

If you want, I told him, you can punch me since you got spanked.

Mark didn't want to punch me, besides, even if he did, I was bigger and it wouldn't hurt.

So I said that Danny could punch me for him.

No. Mark wanted Danny to punch David, because it was David's fault for being a pussy.

I kid you not. Mark, so little that snot still rimmed his nostrils half the time, called David a pussy, and then asked his older brother to sucker punch David in the stomach.

No one punched David, but it was made clear to him that if he ever ratted one of us out again, Danny would not only punch him, everyone else probably would, too.

David lived in terror for the next couple of weeks, until the back tire on his bike went flat and he was heard to utter, "God *dammit!*"

Sometimes, it just pops out and there's no putting it back. Swear words happen. It's not personal.

It was a good thing for him that my mother was at least partially aware of playground rules later in the year when he called her a bitch under his breath. She didn't storm off in a huff of I'm-Telling-Your-Mother; she simply waggled her finger in his face and told him in no uncertain terms that it was inappropriate language and she never wanted to hear it again, Or Else.

He nearly wet himself at the idea of "or else" and ran home. She watched him, and with a sigh said, "He really is a little fucker, isn't he?"

Go Mom.

54.

Our freshman year.

Ev had token ownership of our mother's battered and creaky fifteen year old cast-off Ford; they tried to trade it in when they bought the station wagon, but the $100 offered by the dealership was, Dad sneered, an insult he refused to acknowledge. They'd keep the car and let Ev drive it, as long as she paid for her own insurance.

I think she paid the premiums once. Gas was gifted on the promise that she would pick Steven and me up from school once or twice a week, when Mom was otherwise occupied with friends or whatever book was currently holding her interest.

Ev agreed to the arrangement enthusiastically. A car and gas and all she had to do was show up once or twice a month to cart someone else home. How much better could it get?

Every time I walked out the side door of

the language arts hallway and saw that rusted out heap waiting, I prayed it would fall apart before I was old enough to drive. As the queen of hand me downs, it was surely going to be mine if it held up.

One cold December afternoon Ev waited with the car running, trying to tease what little heat she could from the engine. It worked sporadically, and if she cut the engine the heater might take the entire ride home to kick back on.

I climbed into the front seat as fast as I could, lest any warmth escape, slamming my door and reaching for my seat belt in one movement.

Ev reached for the gear shift and started to roll away from the curb.

"Hey." I dropped my books to the floor. "Wait for Steven. He has to come from the other side of the school."

"Orphan Boy can find his own way home."

"What, you can't give your own brother a ride?"

"Well, if I had a brother, I would."

"What the hell?"

"The little leech has two legs. He can walk home. It's not that far and the fresh air will do him good."

"Yeah, if it wasn't too far Mom wouldn't have told you to pick us up."

"Why don't you take the bus, anyway?"

There was no bus, and she knew that. She'd been driven to school and picked up every weekday afternoon of her life. There had never been a bus that picked up kids from our neighborhood, and there would never be a bus. There were only vans of carpooling Moms and Dads, who complained through gritted teeth that their tax dollars could be spent on at least one school bus that would pick kids up closer than ten miles away.

"If you want to keep driving this car," I said, "you'd better wait for him."

"Like they'd take it away."

"In a heartbeat. Mom told you to pick *both* of us up. You don't get to decide to leave one of us behind."

"It's my car, Sam. I can do whatever I want with it."

I leaned against the car door and glared at her. "You really want to walk in the door and tell Mom you just didn't feel like giving Steven a ride home? That you thought he'd be better off walking in the cold, even though she implicitly told you to pick both of us up? That you decided that even though the only reason you get to drive this car is because you promised you'd do exactly that?"

"I said I'd pick you up. I never said anything about him."

"God, you're a bitch."

She didn't have time to dispute it; Steven

opened the back door and slid onto the seat.

"What?" he asked when Ev looked sideways at him.

"She thinks we should walk," I said, still glaring at her.

"It's five freaking degrees out!"

"Apparently that doesn't matter."

"Hey, Ev, if you want to walk, I'll drive the car home."

She sucked in a deep breath and put the car back into drive, jerking away from the curb so hard the wheels skipped and squealed.

"So what's the deal, Evil-lyn?" he asked, leaning forward. "Do we stink, or did you have better plans?"

She ignored him.

"Ah. The silent treatment. Sam, do you recall if she's said more than ten words to me in the last two years?"

"No. How'd you get so lucky?"

"Must be part of my natural charm."

"You need to teach me, oh wise one."

"My charm or how to be like Ev?"

"Take your pick."

"I don't think you can learn the essence of my natural charms. But to be like Ev, you need to eat a heaping bowl of Frosted Bitch Flakes for breakfast every day."

"Naw. That makes you fat."

"Shut up," Ev seethed.

"Be honest," Steven said, leaning back

into the seat, "You just didn't want me along for the ride."

Ev was grinding her teeth together, but she didn't say anything.

"You don't have to like me. You don't have to talk to me. You don't even have to acknowledge my existence. But for cripe's sake, at least be human about it. By the time I walked home in this my nads would be frozen solid."

"You know, if you would wear a jacket," I started.

"It wouldn't cover my nads. And I may need those someday."

Ev drove home at a good twenty miles over the speed limit, silent the rest of the way, and after Steven and I got out of the car she took off in a rubbery squeal.

"Well that went well," he muttered.

I didn't tell him she'd said he wasn't her brother. But I never forgot it, and it colored the way I saw her after that. She wasn't just Ev, the lazy, socially backwards sister. She was Super Bitch, and I don't think I ever gave her the chance to shake that image in my head.

55.

"It was so easy for you," Ev said. "It was like the Sibling Fairy showed up at the door one day and gave you the brother you'd always wanted. You didn't stop to think of what him being there meant."

I knew on the surface what it meant; it meant there had been some infidelity going on, and Steven was the proof. I let her go on instead of pointing out the obvious.

"Nothing you or I ever did was anything special, you know that, right? Kelly got pregnant and the whole world revolved around that for so long—I walked on egg shells for *years* because I didn't want to do anything that would hurt everyone so much. I didn't go out with my friends all that much and I was afraid to date..." She swallowed hard, choking back on tears that had reddened her eyes. "All I wanted was a goddamned normal life, and it was just about to happen. I was making new friends and Mom and

Dad had started to relax a little and I was only going to be a teenager for a couple more years."

"And then came Steven," I mused.

"Then came Steven, and they were back to being uptight and tense, and I knew I was never going to get to be a real teenager. They were so focused on him that you and I were on the backburner again, and if we'd made one mistake it might have blown the family apart."

"So you stopped trying to make friends?"

"I stopped thinking I could just go hang out. After a while I didn't have friends anymore and after high school I didn't even know how to make friends."

"But that wasn't Steven's fault."

"I don't care, Sam. If he hadn't been there, you and I would have had a chance to just grow up like everyone else and not worry about every little step we took."

"I never worried, Ev."

"Well I did enough worrying for both of us, then. We got cheated. We shouldn't have had to live with getting our lives all stirred up over a kid who never should have been born in the first place. And then like that he was gone! We went through all that and they didn't even keep him!"

"He wasn't an errant puppy, Ev. They didn't give him away; they let him go live with his Uncle."

"Did you know that?" she asked sharply. "I didn't know that. As far as I knew it was just 'Hey, we're moving but we're not taking the boy with us.' All I saw was Dad leaving his son behind. It might have helped if they'd told us he was going to live with his uncle and aunt."

I admitted, for all that time I thought he'd been tossed out like the trash too. But I didn't think Ev had cared; I thought she'd been happy he was gone. After all, he was never her brother.

"He was just some kid to me. But come on, Sam. How were we supposed to trust them after that? How did we know they weren't going to just shove us out the door if we ever became an issue for them? How were we supposed to feel safe in our own home?"

"I never thought of it that way, I guess."

"And Kel...you think she wanted to get married? They *made* her do that, Sam. She did something half the kids in America do, and BOOM she's out the door and gone. Then Steven was gone. How could you trust them after that?"

I didn't know. I was too young when Kel hopped off to her shotgun wedding and years of martial misery to think much about the implications. And I never tied the logic of that with the belief that Steven had been left behind.

But somewhere inside, I was a bit like Ev; I think I stopped trusting them.

"Is that why you're still living here, Ev?" I asked. "Are you waiting to trust them?"

"I don't know why I'm still here."

"Don't you want to be on your own?"

She shrugged. "I don't get along with people, Sam. I don't know how. I get a job and think everything is fine until I realize people are laughing at me behind my back, or setting me up to be the fall guy for their missteps—then I don't know what to do or how to fight back without getting..." she trailed off, shaking her head.

"Bitchy?"

"No one taught me how to be an adult," she said softly. "They taught me how to be afraid, and to not be sure of myself. And now no one is happy, and somehow it's all my fault."

"Growing up isn't optional, Ev."

"Yes. It is. Growing old isn't, but there are a million ways you can avoid growing up."

"But you didn't want to avoid it."

"Would you want to be fifty years old and living with your mommy and daddy because you can't get your shit together?"

"I still don't get how this is Steven's fault."

"If he hadn't shown up when he did, everything would have been so different."

"You would have had the chance to grow up."

"I think so."

"So he wasn't your brother."

"I hated Steven," she admitted. "It wasn't his fault, but it was his physical presence that threw everything out of whack. I know his being there was Dad's fault, and we should have known about him, but that doesn't mean I had to like him. He wasn't my brother. You don't have to like that, either."

"No, I don't."

"And it doesn't have to make any sense that I'm still mad as hell that they left him behind when we moved."

"No, it doesn't."

"I know he was your brother, Sam. And I really do respect that you loved him..."

"...but why didn't it seem like I loved you as much?"

She nodded.

"Because you *were* there, Ev. Steven got put up on a pedestal because I was pissed off he was left behind, too. But I always loved you."

"You just didn't like me."

"No, sometimes I liked, you too. But until now I didn't understand why it seemed like you were so lazy and spiteful."

"I don't know how to be any different."

"And I'm sorry if saying you're lazy and

spiteful hurts your feelings. I don't intend to."

"Truth hurts."

"You know Mom and Dad never intended to shove you to the side, right? They know they made some whopper mistakes, but they didn't know how to fix them."

"I don't know that they tried."

"They did the best they could. And you know, someday Simon may sit down with Tucker and bitch about the same things. Why parents suck so much. We hurt our kids, Ev. We don't mean to, but it's part of being human."

"Would you ever lie to Simon about something so big?"

Do lies of omission count? "No. But I probably swing the other way. I tell him the truth about almost everything, when there are some things I should probably keep to myself."

"Only almost everything?"

"He doesn't know about Steven," I said. "My lame excuse for that is that I was always afraid it would make him hate his grandparents."

"Will it?"

"I don't know. Now that I know the truth, when I tell him it might just make him understand them a little more."

"And if it doesn't?"

"That's the chance I have to take."

"What if he hates you for never telling him?"

"That's another chance I have to take."

That was easy to say, that I had the guts to take that chance, but Ev didn't seize on it.

"The last time I saw Simon he was only five or six years old, wasn't he? He grew up well."

"I think he was closer to ten, but yeah, he grew up just fine. It took him a while to figure out that a full time job wouldn't kill him, but he's doing just fine."

"Grown up."

I nodded.

"You did a better job with him than was done with us, I think."

"Not better, just different."

"He trusts you, doesn't he? And you trusted him enough to push him out the door when it was time. You did a better job, Sam. I don't see what's wrong with admitting that."

"It's probably because I'm seeing our parents in a slightly different light tonight. Two days ago I would have agreed without thinking about it."

"We weren't raised to be nice people. I don't know how you and Kel managed it. You are nice people, you know. I wish I knew how to be one."

"Wanting it is the first step, Ev."

"No, I think I have to want it when I'm

sober. I'm not exactly sober tonight."

"You'll still want it in the morning."

"I hope so. Because the truth is, our parents aren't getting any younger, and some day they're going to die, and I don't have a clue how to exist on my own. I have to figure that out, and I think the first thing I need to do is learn how to be nice."

"Or just civil."

"I'll take whatever I can, Sam, nice or civil, as long as it comes with a steady paycheck and real people to talk to once in a while."

56.

When I was six, Ev was outgrowing her massive collection of Barbie and Ken dolls. She kept them lined up on the window sill of her bedroom, half of them naked, all of them sitting with legs jutted out straight.

I left them alone; I had no interest in Barbie, and Ken didn't come with army clothes the way down-the-street-Danny's G.I. Joes did, so there was little for me to even consider in her little plastic coven. Once in a while I noticed them as I passed her open door, their creepy little eyes staring out into nothingness, but that was it. I certainly didn't want to play with them.

Then came the day Ev announced that it was time to box them up; she hadn't touched one in "forever" and she wanted the window sill for other, more important things.

"Like what?" Dad asked.

We were at the dinner table, the Place of All Pronouncements. Ev shrugged; she wasn't sure of anything other than it was time for the dolls to go.

"Give them to Sam," Kel snickered. She knew just how much I didn't want to play with dolls; it was funny in an I'm-A-New-Teenager kind of way.

Before I could stick my tongue out at her, Mom was nodding in agreement. "That's a wonderful idea! Sam could use some new things to play with."

I was horrified; I know my eyes went wide and I scrambled to think of ways to protest without getting into trouble.

Give me new toys, sure, but not dolls!

"Sam," Dad said, "will just run over them with her bike, or rip the legs off for the fun of it. She and those other little hoodlums she plays with will bake them with magnifying glasses or tie them to their bikes and ride with the dolls bouncing on the ground. Ev's entire collection would wind up ruined."

Ev shrugged. She didn't care.

"Oh, it would not. Sammy knows how to play with dolls."

Before Dad opened his mouth, I didn't think I did. I swallowed my food and said, "Sure."

Mom's mouth practically dropped open. Sammy wanted dolls to play with. Sammy wanted *girl* toys.

Dad winked at me.

Within a month I learned that Barbie's

head looks a bit freaky without hair, and that if dragged around the block six or seven times, her boobs will wear off and leave two neat pencil sized holes. Ken's nether regions will melt in a smelly black smear when exposed to a small magnifying glass in the sun, and his decapitation can be completed by setting him on the top of a t-ball stand, and beating the hell out of him with a bat.

If Ev was upset about the maiming of her former vast collection, she didn't say anything. Our mother, upon the discovery of a box filled with headless, hole-riddled, and bald dolls, sighed hard and then deposited the remains in the trash without another word in praise of Sam and her newfound interest in gender appropriate playthings.

A few months later, when I turned seven, I was gifted books and a giant box of crayons—not a doll to be seen—and a basketball from my Dad.

"She likes to dribble," he explained to my exasperated Mom. "It'll be good exercise."

He used the same logic two years later when he gave me this odd contraption consisting of four heavy duty bungee cords held together with handles on either end. "Terrific exercise," he said. "She can build a little muscle."

My mother warned me with a heavy sigh, that I wasn't going to develop massive muscles, no matter how much weight I lifted or pulled or pressed.

Three days later when the right handle slipped out of my hand and smacked me in the side of the head, leaving my ear a bloody mess, she wasn't especially sympathetic. I was in agony, tears rolling down my face, and she shrugged it off.

"You're not dying, Sam. That's what you get for playing with things you shouldn't."

My Dad noted the bruise and said, with a modicum of pride, "That'll happen. Hold on better next time."

Nine years old and I learned; shit happens, you get bloody, but you live. It's not always worth crying about.

Later that year, at nine years old, I ruined Christmas for Ev. We'd enjoyed the Santa charade all along; we got presents from Mom and Dad, stockings stuffed with candy, and two or three unwrapped gifts from the Jolly Old Elf placed just so under each stocking.

There was also a ritual to Christmas morning: no matter how early we woke up, no one was to get out of bed until we heard Dad stomp down the hallway to the sound of jingle bells, bellowing *Get those reindeer off of my roof!* Once the front door banged shut—because, obviously, he had gone outside to chase the fat guy off the roof—we jumped out of bed and ran into the living room, ready to cave into holiday greed and gift giving merriment.

We got to examine the gifts Santa had left, and we poured the contents of our stockings out onto the floor, shrieking with anticipation over brand new toothbrushes and packs of gum and candy, knowing that we were soon going to shred the wrapping paper on all those gifts under the tree.

The first gift each of us opened was always labeled "from Midnight," our crotchety cat, and was always something small that she could play with—feathers on a string, jingle balls, peanuts in the shell. Even the first year we had the cat I understood that it was Mom's way of giving Midnight a few Christmas presents, too, without making Dad's eyes roll over spending money on a walking bag of farting fur.

After the fiasco of Christmas at eight, when everything I got was clothing my mother wanted me to wear, in spite of her assurances that she had been positive I would love it all, my long held suspicions that Santa was not real were confirmed.

Santa would not give me pink dresses and pink tights. Santa would bring me the baseball glove I had begged for all summer.

So I admitted it. At Thanksgiving dinner, when Dad asked what we wanted from Santa, I rolled my eyes and groaned, "Come on, aren't we all too old for that?"

He grinned slyly, Mom looked a little disappointed, Kel was surprised, and Ev was just pissed.

"What makes you say that?" Dad pressed.

"A fat guy going down a chimney that even Midnight couldn't get down?"

"But he's magic," Ev hissed.

"No one has enough magic to go to five hundred billion houses in one night."

"The whole world doesn't celebrate Christmas, Sammy," Kel said, as nicely as she could. "And he has over twenty fours hours, really, if you think about it."

"Well, if Santa was real, he wouldn't bring me *pink* clothes, and that's what happened last year!"

Dad snorted back a laugh as he took a bite of a roll.

"Besides," I added, "I'm nine! If I said I believed in Santa much longer, everyone would think I was stupid or something."

"There's no 'or something,'" Ev said.

Sheepishly, Mom said, "I'm sorry about the clothes, Sam. And I'm sorry if knowing about Santa hurts."

"I've known for a long time, like three years."

"But you didn't have to *admit* it," Ev seethed.

"Why does it matter?" Dad asked.

"Because now we won't get as many presents!"

Truthfully, if I had considered that angle I might have kept my mouth shut.

"It's not about the presents," Kel said. "It's just more fun when someone believes in Santa."

"It is, too, about the presents."

"Well, I got news for you," I said to Ev. "There's no Easter Bunny, either, so you can count on not getting a basket full of candy next year."

She started to push away from the table, but stopped when Dad raised an eyebrow. "What's wrong with you, anyway? Why do you always have to ruin everything?"

Dad started to open his mouth, but I shrugged and replied, "That's my job as the baby sister."

"Nothing is ruined," Mom said with a sigh. "We'll still have stockings and it will still be fun."

"I bet Ev thinks Midnight really shops for those presents every year, too," I snickered.

"Be nice," Dad said, still trying not to smile.

Ev was not amused. "This isn't funny! She *does* ruin everything, it's not fair."

"What has she ruined?" Dad asked.

"EVERYTHING! She doesn't like anything she's supposed to and it ruins stuff for us."

"Maybe we need new traditions," Kel offered. "Something to take the place of opening Santa's presents."

"Like?" Dad asked.

"I don't know...I'm just thinking out loud. It doesn't really matter, and it doesn't ruin Christmas." She glanced at Ev as she said that.

"Maybe *Santa*"—for Ev's sake I had to say it snottily— "can still buy three extra presents, but before Christmas, and we can give them away to those marine guys that stand out in the mall."

Before Dad point out that they already donated toys, Mom said, "You could each pick something out. We could make an afternoon of it, and go to lunch together."

Mom, I learned over the years, liked any excuse to go out to lunch.

Ev muttered, "Oh joy," but Kel was beaming with excitement and started making plans about what she would buy and could we all wear matching clothes when we shopped together (um, no.)

We declared a new tradition had been born, and it probably would have been, if that hadn't been Kel's last Christmas as a typical teenager.

"Did you ever think," Steven said when I related the tale later, "that maybe Ev was upset because she hadn't figured out the whole Santa thing yet?"

"Dude, she was twelve years old."

"This is Ev we're talking about."

"She's rude, crude, and socially unacceptable, but I don't think she's stupid."

"I didn't say she was stupid. But she is pretty naïve most of the time."

"You know, that's pretty much like you or me still believing in Santa."

"For all you know, I still did, up until you just *ruined* it for me."

"I ruin everything," I told him. "Didn't you get that memo?"

It was our second Christmas together; the tree was up in the living room, and lights had been strung around it, but no one had ventured far enough into the holiday spirits to bother putting ornaments on it. We were sitting on the couch staring at it, debating whether or not we'd get in trouble if we started hanging them without parental permission.

Not that Ev would want to help, but God forbid I ruin something for her again.

"You know," he said, "I thought getting a present from the cat last year was pretty odd."

"But did you notice it was really for her? Midnight is a selfish shopper."

"Who isn't?"

"What about your Mom?" I asked. I knew little about her and nothing about their traditions. For all I knew Christmas was a foreign concept to him, ignored as a pagan based ritual celebrated only by those less religious.

And Steven was fairly religious.

"She loved Christmas. It started the day after Thanksgiving and went right up until New Year's Eve. She decorated the house like it was the freaking North Pole and had tons of little surprise presents just about every other day."

Christmas Day, however, there were always only three gifts; Jesus had only gotten three, so Steven was only getting three. There was one big one (gold) and two smaller presents (Frankincense and Myrrh) and a stocking filled with candy, but that was it. They started the day at church, came home for presents and pancakes, and then spent the day with his uncles and cousins.

Dad would visit a couple of days before Christmas and they would go out to dinner— just the two of them—and then went home to open the gifts Dad had brought, presents that always elicited a "but that's too expensive" from his mother. Steven usually got Dad a shirt and tie, or books, and Dad always had a token gift for Steven's mother, chocolate or a basket of bath oils.

"It was fun," he mused. "One of the few times every year that I had them both in the same room, talking with me instead of about me."

"You miss seeing the rest of your family on Christmas?"

He nodded.

"So go this year."

He thought about it for a moment. "It might hurt Dad's feelings. Besides...I'm afraid to ask."

Mom rounded the corner right then, and as she dropped an armload of clothes to be donated to Goodwill onto a chair, she asked, "Afraid to ask what?"

"Steven wants to go see his cousins on Christmas," I said before he could protest. "He used to go over there every year and he's going to miss it if he doesn't get to this year."

"It's all right, really," Steven sighed.

Mom waved him off. "Steven, it's fine. I'll call and see if they wouldn't mind a little visitor on Christmas afternoon. Your Dad would be happy to drive you over, I'm sure."

"What about church?" I pressed. "He didn't get to go last year and he always went with his mom."

She was looking right at him. "I wouldn't dream of taking that away from you. Do you want to go alone, or would you like some company?"

"I'll go," I volunteered.

"Sam in church. Hell really will freeze over," he snickered.

"We can get up and ride our bikes," I said. "If you want me to go, that is."

"That'd be cool."

So we went. Before Dad could stomp down the hall, chasing the reindeer away, Steven and I were riding our bikes towards the First Church of Christ, freezing and trying to not complain about it.

Afterwards we went home to open presents with everyone else, then after a sleepy lull he headed towards his uncle's house for Christmas dinner; on the way out the door Mom handed him a basket filled with home-made fudge and cookies, "For your cousins."

I thought she was simply being polite; you go to someone's house on a holiday, you don't show up empty handed. She made killer fudge, and it was an appropriate gift for a kid to bring to a family gathering.

Looking back, I don't think it was politeness or common courtesy, or even for his cousins. I'm pretty sure it was for him.

When he came home that evening, he bounded into my room and dropped onto my bed with a bounce, then handed me a brightly wrapped package.

"It's from my Uncle Rob," he said. "I told him how you were the one who asked your Mom if I could spend Christmas with them. He wanted you to have this."

It was a journal, three hundred lined, blank pages wrapped in a fake leather cover.

"I must have told him you liked to write,"

Steven said when I opened it.

It was perfect; there were no cute kittens or pink flowers on the cover, and there was no flimsy lock wrapped around the edges with DIARY embossed in cheap gold flake. It was simple and black, understated and very much me.

"Dude, it looks kind of like a Bible."

"Yeah...you can carry that around and no one will mess with it because they won't know it's a journal. They'll think you just got all Jesus freak on them."

I never questioned how a total stranger would know me well enough to really understand what I would like the most, or how his family would know I was so much not the girl that a simple black journal would thrill me right down to my toes.

57.

"How could I have not known that Vice Principal Browning was your uncle? It's not like you never biked off to visit that side of your family."

I dunno. Surely I uttered the words "Uncle Rob" once or twice.

"You think I'd remember that."

That doesn't mean you could connect the dots. There are a lot of men named Robert out there. Or maybe you just repressed the knowledge that I had other family out there. People who didn't treat me like I was invisible.

"Ev is Ev. And I still can't figure out why you never told me you were living with family and not some random strangers Dad picked out of a classified ad in the newspaper."

You weren't exactly receptive to that part of my life.

"I wanted you living with me...I don't know. I know I wanted you to be happy."

You wanted me to be happy, but in your home. I was happy enough in mine.

"I get that now."

We were kids, Sam. We were allowed to be a little selfish about what we wanted.

"And you wanted to live with your uncle and cousins."

It was easier.

"I know."

It wasn't anyone's fault. And it's not like we didn't try. Almost everyone tried.

"You divorced your dad, didn't you?"

For all intents and purposes, I suppose so. It may have been a mutual separation.

"So Ev seems to think. She who hated you so much was mad as hell that Dad didn't fight to keep his son."

So are you.

"But for different reasons, I think. I just wanted my brother there. Ev saw something bigger."

And you think she might be on to something?

"I think we're too dismissive of our surly sister."

It's like someone gave her a box of nails and a hammer, and she hit the head on each one with every strike. Is that what you're thinking?

"Something like that."

Just because someone hates their life, that doesn't mean they don't see what's going on around them.

"I always thought she was just innately bitchy. But she's scared. Terrified."

Seeing your parents manipulate their children can do that.

"She blames Dad."

And you always excuse him, while laying blame at your Mom's feet.

"I'm still not sure I'm wrong about him. I still think he just did what he thought was the right thing to do. Just because he thought it was right, that doesn't mean it was."

You're going to hurt your brain, thinking in circles.

"Did he let you go, or did he just wimp out?"

There's the big question.

"He says if he had known you were going to die in a few years, we would have stayed in Texas. I don't doubt he meant that."

Do you doubt I was better off living with my uncle?

"No. I hated it, but I know it was better for you."

But you wish he'd fought harder.

"I honestly don't know if he fought at all. Once you were under his roof, who was it that acted as your parent? Who was it who stormed down to the school on your behalf? Who was it who hid in the bleachers during your games, even when you didn't want them there? Jesus…who cried for you while you visited your mother's grave?"

Who fought for my life at the very beginning?

"I'm having a hard time wrapping my brain around that one. There's a chance you might not have lived at all, if not for my mother standing up for yours."

Kind of puts a whole new spin on things, eh?

"Dad might not have fought for you, but she let you go."

Amazing thought.

"So what do I think now? That my family is just one giant ball of screw up?"

Maybe it's time to stop thinking that your family is a special kind of screw up. Your family is what it is, and there's no changing it.

"I'm not sure I'm ever coming back, you know."

Well, that's something, because a few days ago you were sure you were never coming back.

58.

We sat and watched as Dad shuffled out the front door for a doctor's appointment, Mom right behind him with a steadying hand at his back. I was a little taken back by how old he looked, how small his steps had become and how fragile they both seemed.

"He's eighty three years old," Kel pointed out. "I think slowing down is inevitable."

I could think of a dozen people his age that hadn't slowed down yet and showed no signs of it, but I kept it to myself. He had outlived just about everyone in his family, so the micro-steps were a small price to pay.

"He's too damned stubborn to die," Ev sniped.

"So...what? Now you hate Dad?"

"I don't hate him." She took a deep breath, her forehead wrinkled as she considered her next words. "All right, this is out of the blue, but I've thought about it a lot.

Remember when you got your driver's license? How the car you'd been promised since I got Mom's old beater never materialized?"

"That was my fault," Kel said. "With Tucker and me...they just couldn't afford it."

"Bull. They forked over the cash for a car. Steven got it. Sam had the promise but Steven got the car."

I knew he'd gotten a car when he turned sixteen; I had assumed his uncle paid for it, and I admit, the thought that he got the car I'd been promised stung a little bit.

"It's not like I didn't have a car at my disposal," I said, hoping I sounded more generous than I was feeling at the moment. "I don't remember not being allowed to use Mom's car."

"But that's not the point. Steven got *your* car, Sam."

I shook my head. "He got *a* car. What makes you think he got mine?"

"Because," Ev replied, "it's one of the things Mom feels guilty about. You both hit sixteen at the same time and Dad was only going to buy one car, and he thought it was more important for Steven to have one."

Immediately, I knew why. "Because he was a boy. Boys need cars to impress their friends and to drive their girlfriends around."

"Dad was backwards that way," Kel said.

"You got a car," I pointed out to Ev.

"I'm sure he didn't presume I'd have a boyfriend driving me around," she said bitterly. "And letting me have it meant Mom didn't have to always be the one to take you places. If Kel had still been at home, the car would have been hers."

"Dad's a product of his upbringing," I said.

"Stop excusing him so much. You got screwed left and right and I don't think you know it."

I knew it. I chewed on it for years. "We all got screwed, Ev. I've been mad as hell for years about really stupid things, but now I'm not so sure it was anyone's fault. You have kids and you do the best you can."

She was shaking her head. "They did what was easiest."

"And maybe that was their best."

"It wasn't enough."

Kel leaned forward, her elbows digging into her knees. "Ev has a point," she said. "We were all hosed on things we shouldn't have been. I know I try to not think about it, but…"

"So what's the parental fat you chew on?" I asked.

She didn't hesitate. "The biggest mistake of my life was getting married when I was seventeen. I didn't want to, and never should have."

"You wanted an abortion?" Ev asked,

making an Ev-leap from not wanting to get married to not wanting the baby.

"I was seventeen," Kel said. "I don't know what I wanted most, but getting married was not it."

I couldn't imagine life without Tucker, the games we played on the front lawn, and said so.

"I don't *want* to imagine life without him," Kel said. "Tucker wasn't the mistake. He came when he was supposed to come."

"You should have been allowed to stay at home, have Tucker, and then had help while you finished high school," Ev said firmly. "You shouldn't have had to struggle."

"Hard call, really," I said to no one in particular.

"I didn't mind most of the struggle. A little financial help might have been nice, but they couldn't."

Ev sneered at that. "Bullshit. You didn't have to work full time while slogging through school, Kel. They have money, and a lot of it."

"Retirement," I muttered.

"I know where the money is," Ev said, eyes flashing with anger. "Every damned penny, and how long they've had it. They could have given Kel enough money every month to keep her in school without working and never felt it. They could have paid her rent or even bought her a damned house and never had to blink more than once at the idea of another mortgage."

Kel started to say something, but Ev was on a roll.

"And you," she said to me. "After your accident...they knew you needed a better wheelchair. Mom kept telling him you were stuck at home alone most of the time because yours was too heavy to lift. They could have bought you one without feeling it one bit, but instead they bought furniture. You needed a goddamned wheelchair but he decided they needed to replace crap that was less than five years old. Dad dropped seven thousand dollars without even thinking about it. No one here *needed* a new sofa and kitchen table and recliner, but you needed a lighter wheelchair, and they *knew* it. It was your freaking *independence*, Sam! Not helping you was just another way to keep you from it."

I was rendered speechless; Ev was pissed, and it wasn't about her.

She was pissed off for me.

Kel sighed and said, "Sometimes I hate it when you're right, Ev. I don't think what they do is intentional, but—"

"Not they," she said. "Dad."

"Are you serious?" I asked.

She ticked things off on her fingers. "Dad cheats, he has a kid because of it, and he gets away with it because he was 'depressed.'

That was a load of bullshit, too. He was upset because *Mom* was depressed and he took advantage of it. Dad leaves that kid behind. Dad decides the son needs the car, not the daughter. Dad decided Kel had to get married to salvage family honor, knowing *he* had a bastard son across town. Dad decided Kel would move in when her marriage was over. Before she could blink Dad decided she would move back out. Dad decided I couldn't cut it in college, so I didn't go. Dad decided I wasn't smart enough. Dad decides everything, Sam. Mom goes along with it for whatever reason, probably because at the beginning he decided she would."

"Steven wanted to stay behind," I ventured.

"So what? Who's the parent? When do kids get to make those kinds of decisions? Either be the parent or don't, but don't hang that kind of crap on a kid."

"Did Dad really say you weren't smart enough for college?" Kel sputtered.

"He said it wouldn't be a worthy endeavor, and he didn't want to pay good money for me to waste everyone's time."

"But he paid for Sam to go."

"Just my books," I said, trying to remember back that far. "Community college in California was free back then, and when I transferred, it was on scholarship."

"Plus, Sam was the surrogate son," Ev said.

"What?"

"Face it," she said to me. "You were the closest thing he was ever going to get to having a son living with him. You dressed the part—something he managed to get going when you were a toddler—you acted the part, you had the toughness...he let you go, but only so far."

"Then Sam got married," Kel murmured, mostly to herself.

"Sam got married and it was obvious she wasn't his pretend son. She did something very girl-like. She fell in love, and then had a kid of her own."

"So he yanked the independence right out from under her," Kel said quietly. "No new wheelchair for Sam, because that would mean she could do things for herself."

"I have light bulb moments," Ev mused.

"You think Dad is why you're still here?" I asked Ev. "Did he somehow maneuver that?"

She shrugged. "I learned self-sabotage somewhere."

"And you're going to stop," Kel declared. "You're going to take your big sister's help, which means getting you a job, and you're going to stick with it no matter how bitchy you feel after the third week. And you're getting out of here and into your own apartment."

"I don't know how," she started.

"You are not letting Dad win this one," Kel said. "You are not going to die in this house because he couldn't let you go."

There was a data entry clerk opening at Kel's firm; Kel said she would make sure Ev got the job. When she was ready for an apartment, Kel would make sure she had all the deposits she needed, and enough help to drive her bat-shit crazy.

Kel pointed a finger at Ev and said, "You're a lot smarter than you give yourself credit for. You see things the rest of us don't. Dad was dead wrong, Ev, and don't you forget it."

Ev sank back in her chair. How many times had she been forced to face the unknown, even if it did hold the promise of being exciting and liberating?

She sat there quietly, the fear drawn out in tiny pixels across her face. It was a drum beat in her head. *A real job, a paycheck, someone to keep me from blowing it, a real job…*

Kel was equally quiet, surprised that not only had the offer popped out of her mouth, but that she meant it.

The silence was as loud as it was uncomfortable.

"I'm fat," I said to no one in particular.

Kel let a slip of a laugh out. "What?"

"I'm fat. Just so you know I know it."

"What," Ev asked, "does that have to do with anything?"

I shrugged. "I just thought I'd toss it out there."

"No one cares about your weight, Sam," Ev sighed.

"Unless it's affecting your health," Kel added.

"Or how much pain you're in."

I couldn't believe I'd heard that coming out of Ev.

"I just figured...you know, the elephant in the corner."

"You're fat. I'm a fifty year old toddler. Kel tries too hard to please. We're all leaning a little to the left of perfect. So what?"

I was thinking that I wouldn't mind it as much if my weight was table-fodder after I left, that I would understand if it came up in a less than kind way. Discussing my weight might be less painful than discussing whether or not they'd ever see me again.

"You got out, Sam. We're still here but you got out."

"Granted, you ate your way out," Ev snickered.

She made me laugh. For the first time in years, perhaps ever, Ev made me laugh out loud.

59.

A day later Ev asked, as she stared at the table, "If I move out, what happens to Mom?"

"Mom will be fine," Kel assured her.

"She won't have anyone to talk to."

"She has Dad."

Ev looked up; her eyes were tinged with red, but it wasn't the fear of leaving she was fighting back. "I don't think she does. I think if she's here alone, her life is going to be so quiet that she'll lose it."

"So you want to stay? What happened to getting a life of your own?"

"I still want a real job, Kel, but I can't leave her here alone. She needs me."

My impulse was to tell Ev that she was falling back on old excuses; she had the chance to get out, she needed to take it.

But, I wasn't sure that she was wrong. If she moved out, Mom would live at the kitchen table with her magazines and Dad would live in the den with his newspapers and books, and rarely would the two be in the same room for more than three minutes at a time.

Before he retired and took up the hobby of sitting and reading all day long, every day, they were social creatures, going out with friends; he fished and bowled, she quilted with a group of women who spent more time laughing and gossiping than they did actually sewing, and she went on afternoon-long shopping trips with other wives.

When he retired, though, they slowly gave up socializing, and as they got older most of their friends died off. Eventually she stopped going out and stayed home, reading magazines with Ev.

"What do *you* want?" Kel asked Ev.

"I want the job, I want to meet people and figure out how to have friends again," Ev said.

"But?"

"But I can't move out. Someone has to stay here."

"So Mom has someone to talk to."

"So Mom doesn't go insane."

"But—"

"She's right," I sighed. "Mom needs someone to talk to, even if it's to complain about everyone else. And she's going to need help with Dad sooner rather than later."

Kel sucked in a deep breath, and nodded.

"I can work," Ev pointed out, "and invite Mom to meet me for lunch a couple of times a week. You know how much she would like that. And then I'll be home at night for her to talk to. At least this time around, I'll know why I'm staying."

"All right, then."

"You're disappointed," Ev said.

"No. I'm actually impressed. It doesn't matter if you stay here, as long as you have a reason, and I think being there for Mom is a pretty decent reason."

"Reasons are better than excuses," Ev said, looking at me, a smile tugging at the corners of her mouth.

Kel turned to me. "What about you, Sam?"

"I can't really stay and talk to Mom. I have a plane to catch tomorrow."

"Funny. Is it going to be another fifteen years before we see you again?"

In that moment, I couldn't imagine waiting until I was sixty years old to see my sisters again.

I'd lost my excuses for staying away, and sitting at the table that I hated so much, I had at least two reasons for coming back.

60.

"All my oddities...those were never about Steven," my mother said. "I know that. I was flakey before he came to live with us and flakey afterwards. He wasn't why I was so out there half the time."

We were in Ev's car, heading towards the airport, discussing the Why of Sam Doesn't Want To Be Pretty. How was it possible to be agonizing over getting Sam into a dress one day and fine with jeans the next? Why lament over Sam's flood of tears at the idea of a ribbon in her hair, and getting it cut boy-short a week later? And especially why was she so afraid that Sam would be, you know, *that*.

"I'd be fine with it now, you know," she admitted with a slip of a sigh. "You live and you learn. All I ever wanted was for you to be happy, but being—you know—that would make life hard and uncomfortable, and I had no way of knowing that people would change so much by the time you were grown up."

Uncomfortable for whom I didn't ask.

"Forty years ago, you just did everything you could to make sure your children grew up..."

"Normal?" I finished for her.

"Well, yes. We didn't know it was normal. Everyone thought it was a choice, but I couldn't see how anyone could possibly choose that for themselves. People are mean. When they see something that scares them, they get ugly."

"And it scared you."

"I was scared *for* you, Sam. You never wanted anything your sisters did, no dolls, no dresses, and anything pink made you truly angry in a way that actually frightened me sometimes. I couldn't get you to look at clothes in the girl's department for the life of me. Half of the struggle was me wanting you to like girl things, but half of it was just me being outright scared for you."

"And there was Dad, telling you to let me be. He wasn't worried I might be gay?"

She shook her head. "He kept telling me the surest way to make you hate what I wanted was to force it on you, and I couldn't make myself listen. And he said if you were, you know, we'd just have to get over it."

"Very progressive of him."

She been leaned forward, gripping the steering wheel so tightly her knuckles were white, but she brightened and straightened up. "He was, you know. Oh, this sounds so horrible, but do you remember the uproar when that black family, the Bells, was trying to buy the house down the street?"

I nodded; the neighborhood formed a committee, and the agenda was How To Keep The Neighborhood Lilly White. "Everyone was worried their property values would go down."

She sucked in a deep breath. "It was awful. Your dad stood in front of all the people we lived around and socialized with, and told them they were all blind, bigoted, foolish people more interested in the almighty dollar than they were about the fact that integration was going to happen sooner or later, and why the hell not let it happen in our neighborhood now. And why the hell don't we get off our racist asses and welcome them openly, because no one was going to be able to stop them from buying that house."

There was a beer guzzling redneck down who lived down the street—he was the stereotype of white trash, with the stained wife-beater A-shirt and a car up on blocks at the side of his house—whose major contribution to the argument was "Well if we let one move in, they'll *all* want to move in. We don't want our homes to be *dark* or nothing."

Dad seized on that. We could welcome our new neighbors, the same as we welcomed anyone else, or we could be—he pointed at the resident redneck—like him. Did anyone else want to be that?

"That whole thing could have turned so ugly. But your Dad stood up for what was right, long before people understood that it was right."

The Bells moved in, our Resident Redneck moved out. Life in the neighborhood went on peacefully, other than a few block parties that got out of hand. The first major Gibson Drive bash was held to welcome the Bell family, and the last we attended was to wish us well as we moved away.

I don't know if Dad was a step ahead of the times, or simply bending to the inevitable.

There we were, forty years later, basking in the glory of Dad's potential progressiveness, yet wondering why Sam doesn't want to be pretty.

"I never *was* pretty, Mom," I said. "I know that. I *knew* that. I just didn't need to be reminded of it all the time. And by asking me 'don't you want to be pretty?' was the practically the same thing as telling me that I wasn't."

"But you were. Even dressed up in jeans and a t-shirt, people were awed by how pretty you were."

"Then...?"

Sheepishly she admitted, "I wanted you to be my idea of pretty."

"And Dad fought you on it."

"I ran hot and cold, Sam. Happy as a clam one day and upset over nothing the next. On days I was happy, I could have cared less if you were in jeans and dirty sneakers, but on the sad days, I wanted my girls to be my kind of pretty. And when you didn't want to, it was my fault. It had to be my fault."

"Not necessarily."

"I didn't say it was rational. And you know, I am on medication for it now."

"What?" I laughed; it caught me off guard.

"Back then it was just 'my moods.' Now we know better; I'm bipolar and *heavily* medicated."

She seemed almost happy about that.

"Well, moods or not, my preferences were never your fault. If blame has to be heaped on someone...well, Dad is the one who started getting my hair cut short, he's the one who bought me boy's toys and made you let me wear jeans all the time."

"He just saw how you were."

"Or he designed me to be what he wanted—a stand-in for Steven."

"He would never—"

"He would never do it intentionally, the

same way you would never try to intentionally make me feel ugly. And it doesn't matter. I like who I am and how I am. It's just that little girls can be influenced by their fathers, too."

She sighed hard. "Do you really think he wanted you to be a substitute for Steven?"

Ev thought so, but I didn't say it. "If he did, it's fine. If all those little things hadn't happened when they did, I might have been a different person by the time I grew up, Scott wouldn't have wanted a whole lot to do with me, and I wouldn't have Simon. If Dad turned me into this macho version of what I was going to be anyway...it's a good thing."

"If you hadn't met Scott, you might not be in that chair," she said.

"I'll take that over life without him, every time."

"And if we had stayed in Texas, even if Steven had gone to live with his uncle, you wouldn't have met Scott."

I nodded. "I miss Steven. I'd give just about anything for him to be alive and sitting here grumping about his kids and getting bald and fat."

"But?"

"But I wouldn't give up Scott. If you take everything, every single thing, and tell me that I can go back and change it all and have Steven be alive right beside me, but it costs me Scott and Simon, I don't think I could make that choice. It would hurt like hell and I would second guess myself all the time, but to think I would never have them..."

"If you could go back and get Steven to move with us, knowing he was going to die?"

"He was miserable with us."

"So you would let him go."

"I'd have to."

"Would you change anything?"

I didn't know. I wanted to know my brother from the beginning; I wanted to be three years old with Steven, running around the back yard in nothing but underwear. I wanted to know the six year old brother who started guitar lessons and sang so badly at first that his mother wore earplugs. I wanted the teenaged Steven to be able to visit freely, to feel welcome enough that we didn't have to hide behind friends to spend a little time together.

I wanted a lot; I wanted Steven on my terms.

If any one of those things had happened, would I have the life I have, as screwed up as it seemed from my semi-permanent seated position in my sister's car, half a country away from my husband and son?

"Maybe," I told her, "everything really does happen for a reason, and maybe I shouldn't wish so hard to change things."

She gestured towards the back of the

car; my wheelchair was resting between the back of the passenger seat and the rear seat. "You would even keep that?"

"It's been a royal pain in the ass and I keep telling myself I'd give anything to be up on two feet without pain, but I don't know."

"So...you think it happened for some big reason?"

"I've considered that. Maybe to humble me enough to remind me I'm not as perfect as I expect everyone else to be."

"That's kind of warped, don't you think? God's not up there pointing fingers making bad things happen to prove a point. I think God just lets it happen. Bad things have to happen, you know."

"I know. Maybe it was just an accident, and doesn't mean anything more than that."

She sucked in a deep breath.

"What?"

"Fifteen years, Sam-I-Am."

"I know."

"Is this the last time I'll ever see you? Be honest."

"Funny, Ev and Kel wanted to know the same thing. I honestly can't see not coming back."

Linc was waiting for me just beyond the security checkpoint; he had called the night before to let me know he would be there and was flying back with me, and for his troubles he expected me to buy him drinks and pretzels on the plane.

Protests that I could fly all by myself thank you very much were waved off with, "I'm thirsty and I'm cheap, and we're headed in the same direction anyway."

We avoided talking about anything more than "Nice trip?" until the plane was in the air.

"She brought him up first," I mused. "There I was thinking that I was going to blindside my parents demanding answers, and they were handing them out like candy. I didn't get to yell at anyone."

"And you liked what they had to say?"

"It doesn't change much," I said. "I lost my brother twice, Linc. Knowing that my mom loved him doesn't change the pain of that. And now...I have to come to terms with the idea that my Dad may have been a huge tool."

He nodded thoughtfully, just a slight bit on the sober side of tipsy. "We're all tools, Sam."

"All men or all parents?"

"Take your pick."

"I can see your daughter standing there with her hands on her hips, sighing 'God, Dad, you're such a *tool*.'"

"Just wait until she's a teenager and

starts dating. I'll go from tool to asshole in a single roll of her pretty little eyes."

"But at least when she's grown she won't wonder about your intentions. I still don't know if we were all instruments in my Dad's warped little orchestra or if he really was trying hard to do the right thing all the way around."

"He loves you, Sam."

"Well, yeah, I know that."

"Then he always tried to do the right thing by you. The same as you always try to do the right thing by Simon, even when you're wrong and he thinks you're a jerk. The same as my daughter stomping her feet and screaming *it's not fair* when I let her brothers have something she doesn't get...thirty years from now she'll still think it was unfair, but I only do what I do because I think it's the right thing at the time."

"And what did the boys get that she didn't?"

"A TV for their room. They can handle it. They do their homework without fighting about it, they do their chores...she doesn't. When she does those things, I'll think about it."

"God, you bastard," I laughed.

"She'll chew on it forever if she never gets that TV. I can live with that."

I gestured towards the approaching flight attendant. "Last call."

He ordered another drink, and when he had it in hand, he took a long sip from it.

"Tell me," he said when he finally set it down, "can you walk now?"

"What?"

"I just figured getting this visit over with would take the weight of the world off you. Nothing weighing you down now."

"Smartass."

He shrugged. "I'm drunk."

"I do feel lighter," I admitted.

"I wish that was the cure, I really do."

"I know."

"I still miss Steven, too."

"I also know that."

"I knew he wanted to stay in Texas when you moved."

"I figured as much."

"I'm sorry."

"It's all right," I said, watching him drain the cup. "He asked you to keep something to yourself and you did."

He shook his head.

"Linc, he was dying and I didn't tell my parents. Steven asked us to keep some big secrets, and we did it because we loved him."

This time he nodded.

"I'm telling Simon about him," I said. "Hopefully he won't hate me."

"You want me to be there? I have a ton of really good Steven stories."

I almost jumped on it; having Linc there

would be a good buffer, but I wasn't sure it would be fair. "Let Scott and me tell him first, and then you can come over and fill in all the blanks. Hopefully he won't be too pissed off to listen."

"He's not Ev."

I snorted a short laugh through my nose. "Ev's not Ev. Ev would surprise you."

"And Simon won't. He's a good kid, Sam. You raised up a fine young man."

"God, you really are drunk."

But he was right; Simon was fair, and Simon was a decent person. If he held it against us that we kept his long gone uncle a secret, he might be angry, but he'd forgive.

61.

So. Now you know. The detritus of my interrupted life was not your mother's fault, and she tried to care for me in spite of my disinterest.

"I wonder now how much you knew. If you realized she was there at your games, cheering you on. And I wonder if you knew how heartbroken she was when you decided to stay in Texas with your uncle."

I would only know how much she let me see. I was just a kid, Sam.

"I've been looking at everything in black and white all these years. Why the hell do I have such a hard time remembering the good things? Why is it so easy to work up my resentment and dwell on the bad?"

Because you didn't understand?

"How could I understand? I was twelve when you showed up and not quite fifteen when we left you behind. I didn't see how badly there being a mother around that wasn't yours hurt, and I couldn't fathom that Mom acted the way she did because she was confused and a little bit scared herself."

And then there was Dad, pacing on the sidelines.

"Dad, totally clueless. He had no idea what to do with you, either. Now I'm not so sure he really tried, or if it was that he didn't know how to try. Cripes. I'm back to thinking in circles."

I knew he loved me, Sam. You know that. Does anything else matter?

"Everything matters. God, my poor Mom...I blamed her, but I never stopped to think that she was struggling."

You're not supposed to let your kids see all your inner struggles.

"It's not always that easy."

So you at least try to hide it from Simon. And thusly does the circle of life go on. Your mother had her private demons, you had yours. Simon will have his.

"And surely I'll be blamed for most of them."

Maybe half. It's always the mother's fault, you know.

Think you'll miss me when I'm gone?

"You're already gone, bonehead. How could I miss you more?"

I'm not the seed of contention between you and your mother anymore. I'm no longer a reason for you to never see your family again. I'm not a secret from Simon. You don't need me anymore, Sam.

"Bull."

You'll tell Simon more about me. You can talk with your family about me now. Linc will visit, and he can tell Simon all the stupid things we did after you moved away. You won't need to pick at scabs with me when you can do it with people who can actually breathe.

"I'm not sure I'd prefer their company."

Sam.

"Well, I'm really not."

Sam. Let me go. Let me rest. Tuck me away into someplace warm and fuzzy in your brain and in your heart, but let me go.

I watched as the condensation on his Coke can rolled in small drops to the table, puddling in a nice twelve ounce sized rim. I stared at it, trying to come up with something that would tell him he could rest and still pop up on the odd occasions to talk to me, but everything stuck in my throat.

When I looked up, Steven was gone.

About The Author

K.A. Thompson is aware that not too many readers will likely turn the pages once the book is over, but what the hell. If you want to know, she lives in Northern CA with her Spouse Thingy, a psychotic cat that has a much larger fan base that she has, and a goofball cat that could use a healthy dose of Ritalin.

www.ingramcontent.com/pod-product-compliance
Lightning Source LLC
Chambersburg PA
CDIIW021452240626
47154CB00002B/340